Why Me?

A Third Natasha McMorales Mystery

C S Thompson

Why Me?

Published in the U.S. by:

CSThompsonBooks.com
Bristol, TN 37620

ISBN 978-0-9794116-7-0

Although the major characters are all fictional and any resemblance to a real person is accidental and unintentional, many of the places are real and the people one would find there are real as well. Those places include:

In the Bristol Area: Blackbird Bakery, Bristol Herald Courier, Bristol Racket Club, Manna Bagel, Michelangelo's, Perkins, Starbucks at exit 7, State Street, State Street Eats & Treats, Tri-Cities Airport.

In the Abingdon area: Alison's Restaurant, Barter Theater, House on Main, Johnston Memorial Hospital, Martha Washington Inn, Valley Drive, Wildflower Bakery, Zazzy'z.

In the New Orleans area: Acme, Anne Street, Bourbon Street, Café Du Monde, Central Grocery, Felix's, French Quarter, Jackson Square, La Divina, Muriel's Restaurant, Napoleon House, New Orleans Cooking School, New Orleans Jazz National Historical Park, Place D'Armes Hotel, Saint Louis Basilica.

PROLOGUE

It was a little thing but it disappointed him anyway. He wanted to hear the "tink" as he threw the empty beer can on the floor behind the passenger seat of his Mustang. You could never hear that "tink" with the first can because there was nothing for it to hit against, but with each empty after that first one, the chances of hearing the "tink" got better and better. He shrugged. It was his second beer, which meant that it would have to be a lucky toss to hit the first empty. He was lucky about half the time. He could have looked where he was throwing, but that would have broken the rules. His rules. Another rule required that because he had not heard the "tink" he would have to open another can while he sat in his driveway.

He had not planned on drinking on the way home from the Food City. He had promised his wife he would not drink while he drove anymore, but a promise to her did not change anything. A promise to her was just to shut her up. Besides, a cold beer was how you took the edge off after "locking in."

Locking in was what a pilot did once the computer had zeroed in on a target. Locking in did not mean you were going to fire on the target but it did mean that an attack was only a nanosecond away. When you got locked in, your focus on the target was complete and nothing else mattered. If the attack was triggered then destroying your enemy was all that mattered. Who else might get hurt, what it would cost, even your own pain were irrelevant once you were locked in.

He had not been looking for trouble. He was just pulling out of a parking place at the Food City when a punk kid told him, "Get your head out of your ass and watch where you're going." It was true, he had not been looking when he backed up and he did come close to hitting the kid's car. *But nobody talks to me like that,* he told himself, *at least nobody was going to do it twice. That punk would not do it twice. That's for sure.*

He got out of the Mustang and walked over to the punk's car. He walked slowly, taking his time and glancing around the parking lot several times. He was casual and confident, knowing he was being watched, but avoiding looking at the car until he was nearly there.

"What did you say, Shirley?" he asked calmly as he leaned into the open window.

He could see the punk sizing him up. As for the kid, he was the stereotype of a wisecracking stoner: long greasy hair, pale skin, pimples, a baggy black T-shirt with some kind of monster on it, and a cigarette over his left ear.

A nice-looking, well-groomed younger girl sat on the passenger side of the front seat. Her Food City shirt made him think this was the punk's sister. Clearly she was too classy for the stoner.

There were two good-sized kids in the backseat, but a direct stare at each one ensured they would stay where they were.

The punk hesitated, probably concerned about how he looked to his entourage, but a prolonged gaze at the intensity in the eyes that were locked in on him made the decision for him.

That was the moment he had been looking for. The moment his target realized his fate. The last slow exhale and the slump of the shoulders as the eyes went blank. He did not really even need the fight itself; the exhilaration came from the victory.

When he saw the humiliation in the punk's eyes, he asked again, "Come on, Shirley, and tell me, what did you say?"

"Nothing," the punk answered softly.

"That's what I thought."

"That's what I thought," he repeated out loud to himself as he sat in his driveway savoring the memory. As he rubbed his good luck piece, a custom-made gold ace of diamonds amulet hanging from a gold chain around his neck, he finished the third beer. He tossed the empty over his shoulder and waited for the sound.

"Tink."

He laughed. His life could not have been better. Taking the grocery bag under his arm he strolled toward his home. He never saw the person waiting in the shadows by his front door until he felt the arm around his neck. He recognized the sleeper hold, but too late to do anything about

2

it. It was a blessing for him to be unconscious while three of his ribs and his upper right leg were broken with what the doctor said was a blunt instrument, probably the baseball bat lying next to him when he was found.

CHAPTER 1

NATTIE HEARS FROM BOO
(Friday evening)

"Nattie Moreland?" asked the man on the phone.

"Yes," Nattie answered. She had a vague recollection of the man's voice and his unusual accent, but could not quite place him yet.

"Nattie Moreland, the private detective?"

"Speaking. How can I help you?"

The pitch of the voice went up slightly, "It's me, Beauregard Robinette. You came out to my place in Barton Square a few months ago. Do you remember?"

The trip he was referring to was an investigation into a murder that had taken place in the parking lot of the Never Tell Tavern. Other than the murderer, Robinette had been the last person to speak to the victim; additionally he was a witness that placed the victim and Nattie's falsely accused client together just before the murder. Nattie had been fairly convinced that her client was indeed guilty until she interviewed Boo. He had been a counselor in New Orleans before Katrina hit, after which he came to northeast Tennessee to refurbish an old boathouse he inherited from an aunt. Nattie remembered him all right. He was a very large man with long dark thinning hair pulled back into a ponytail, a small gold ring in his left ear, a floral tattoo over his right forearm, and a silk Hawaiian shirt.

"Boo?" she asked tentatively, hoping she remembered his nickname correctly.

Boo laughed. "You do remember."

"I do. You're the counselor from New Orleans who was refinishing that tavern. How are you?"

"Better than I deserve. I sold the Never Tell Tavern."

"Well good for you. You did such a nice job fixing up the interior, it was beautiful. How did the outside turn out?"

"I didn't finish the outside," Boo answered. "Hell! I didn't even start working on it. A woman out of Memphis bought it. She made me an offer I could not refuse."

"So what are you up to now?"

"A little cooking and a little bartending while I keep my eyes and ears open for another opportunity."

"Is that why you called? Do you need me to check into an opportunity around Bristol?"

Boo hesitated. "No, that's not why I called. I'm already here in Bristol."

"Really," she interrupted. "Tell me where you are cooking. I want to come try your red beans and rice. It smelled so good to me that day I came to your place. The man I was with that day, Nathan, raved about it. I know he'll want to know where you are too."

"That's real nice, Nattie. Thank you."

"I mean it," she said, "tell me where you are working. I'll bring my brother too. He loves hot food."

Again Boo was quiet for a moment. When he spoke again, his pace had slowed and his pitch dropped. "Before I tell you where I'm working, let me just tell you why I called."

Nattie realized he had become more serious. "OK."

"The other night a guy came in and threatened the owner of the bar. The guy is a military type. Lean and mean. Real intense. He really shook up my friend."

Nattie just listened.

"Then last night someone broke his leg while he was getting out of his car."

5

"Your boss?"

"No, the guy that threatened him. The military guy is the one with the broken leg," he explained. "I want you to find out who did it."

"You want me to find out who broke his leg?"

"I do."

"Aren't the police going to do that?"

"Of course, but when they start asking questions, they are going to find out that my friend was threatened."

"And that will establish his motive and make him a suspect."

"Exactly."

"Well, I hate to point out the obvious to you, but are you sure he didn't do it?"

"I am. I wasn't with him the whole night, but I just know he could not have done it. It isn't in him to do anything like that."

"And you think the only way to prove he didn't do it is to find out who did?"

"That would do it, don't you think?"

"Naturally," agreed Nattie, "but why not just let the police handle it, Boo? He'll be a person of interest, but they'll figure out that it wasn't him."

"That's not the problem. The problem is that this guy is a real cowboy. He's in the hospital now, but we have to get this solved before he gets healthy because he thinks he has two scores to settle now and that is not going to set well with a guy like him."

"So you want to hire an investigator because you want it solved in a hurry."

"That's right."

"And you thought of me because?"

"Because the man with the broken leg is Frank Lester."

Nattie waited a moment for more information before realizing he had expected that name to mean something to her.

"Frank Lester is Randi Lester's husband," he explained.

Nattie remained silent.

Boo continued. "Frank Lester is a helicopter pilot. While he was doing a tour of duty in Iraq, his wife was keeping company with another man."

A knot began forming in Nattie's stomach.

"The man he threatened is my boss, Nathan Moreland, your ex-husband."

Nattie heard exactly what she expected to hear, but hearing it still caught her off guard. With her left elbow firmly planted on the desk, she cradled her forehead in her hand and wondered, *Why me?*

CHAPTER 2

COOKING WITH MOM
(Saturday morning)

"Does that look right?" asked Ingrid O'Brien, popping a small cube of raw carrot into her mouth. She had diced up one of the five carrots on the cutting board at her end of the kitchen counter.

Looking up from where she was dicing onions on another cutting board at the other end of the counter, Nattie studied her mother. At fifty-five, Ingrid O'Brien was still drawing the attention of young men when she went out. A fitted plaid top and skin-tight blue jeans was her idea of casual at-home attire. Ingrid had the same blue eyes, fair skin, and light freckles as her daughter, and they were both on the shortish side. Ingrid's rich auburn hair and Playboy centerfold body, however, were where they differed.

Why didn't I get your butt? wondered Nattie as she walked past the sink to where her mother stood. "Looks good to me, Mom. According to Delia, you want to cut everything close to the same size so that it all cooks at the same rate."

Delia Davenport was the Food TV celebrity Nattie watched, read, and quoted. Ingrid's skills did not include cooking; therefore, Nattie's early kitchen education came from her grandmother, Vee. Early in her

8

marriage her interest in cooking began when she discovered Delia Davenport. She and Nathan had happened into Zazzy'z Coffee House and Bookstore in Abingdon one afternoon when Delia was there signing copies of her cookbook, *Dining With Delia*. Nathan bought her an autographed copy of the book. The gift rekindled her interest in cooking, which to that point in their marriage had been limited to heating up soup and microwaving popcorn. It was Delia Davenport's recipe for ribollita soup they were working on.

Ingrid smiled and stroked Nattie's cheek with the back of her fingers. "This is nice. I wish we could do this more often."

"We should."

"Lionel tells me you and Nathan may be getting back together."

Stepping back, Nattie sighed. She and her stepfather had never gotten along very well. They were destined to clash since he was the kind of man who had strong opinions and shared them strongly, and she was the kind of woman who was most comfortable around men who were helpless and dependent. But recently, when she had solved a case involving one of the lawyers that worked for him, they had made some peace. In a moment of tenderness between them, she told him that she was still in love with Nathan.

"That is not exactly what I told him, Mom."

"What exactly did you tell him then?" Ingrid's accompanying smile seemed patronizing to Nattie.

Nattie wiped at her cheek.

"Are you crying?"

"Oh heavens, no. It's the onions."

Ingrid eyed her more closely. "Are you sure?"

"Absolutely, Mom. It's the onions and I'd like to get it done so I can wash my hands."

Ingrid nodded and let her daughter go back to the onion board.

"I got new business cards," Nattie offered as a way to change the subject.

"That's nice, dear."

"Yeah," she continued, "I made my name larger on this card."

No response from Ingrid, who concentrated on making all the carrot pieces of equal size.

"Having to explain that I am not Natasha McMorales is getting old."

Nattie could not tell if her mother was still listening or not. Just like old times.

They worked in silence until Ingrid announced, "I'm done. What's next?"

By this time Nattie was cutting up the kale. She handed her mother three zucchinis. "This is the last of the cutting. Make these half-moon slices instead of cubes."

"Is that what Delia says?"

"It is."

Silence returned to the kitchen for another few minutes while all the chopping was completed. The pace changed when the diced-up bacon pieces began cooking in the bottom of the soup pot.

"How long does that have to fry?"

"We're rendering the bacon, Mom. And it should take about five minutes."

"Well while the bacon is rendering, why don't you show me your new business card?"

Nattie retrieved one of her new business cards from her bag hanging over the back of a kitchen chair.

"Very interesting," Ingrid said with enthusiasm as she took the card. "I like the white lettering on the turquoise background."

"Thanks, Mom. That's Kevin's touch. I wanted turquoise lettering on a white card."

Ingrid lowered the business card and looked her daughter in the eye. "Did he talk you into this design or did he just do it?"

They laughed together. No answer was necessary.

The next step in making the rebuilt soup was to add all the spices, broth, crushed tomatoes, and the vegetables minus the kale and navy beans. This step would take seven to ten minutes. Nattie adjusted the heat under the soup pot.

"Let's sit down and talk," Ingrid suggested, picking up a mug of coffee and taking a seat at the breakfast table.

The phrase made Nattie flinch. The last time Ingrid said "let's sit down and talk" was the day she told Nattie that her father would not be coming back home anymore. Nattie's father, Nathan Johnson, was a functional alcoholic during most of her childhood. But just before she hit puberty, a critical time for girls and their fathers, he had an accident that cost a little girl her life. His drinking got worse after that and eventually cost him his job and then finally his family. The phrase did not remind her of a banner day in her life.

After refilling her own coffee cup, Nattie took the seat across the breakfast table from her mother, "So, what's the good news?"

"No news, I just wanted to talk." Noticing the suspicious expression on Nattie's face, she added, "Don't give me that look, Natalie. I swear, can't a mother just have an innocent conversation with her adult daughter without it meaning something bad?"

"Of course a mom can do that. Is that what you're doing?"

"OK, OK! I have an agenda. Sue me. I'm just worried about you. Does that make me a bad mother?"

"That depends on what you are worried about and what you do about it."

"I'm worried about your future."

"What about my future, Mother?"

Ingrid placed the Natasha McMorales Detective Agency business card on the table. "I know you are having fun with this now; but please, honey, what kind of life will it be like in ten years? Or twenty years?"

Nattie's eyes rolled involuntarily.

"Seriously, what do you picture it will be like when you turn fifty?"

Natalie grinned. "I was rather hoping to grow into a fifty-year-old body like yours."

Ingrid sat back and took a sip from her coffee mug.

That shut you up, thought Nattie, savoring the victory. Verbal duels with her mother usually left her in knots.

Gazing at the mug she now held with both hands, Ingrid turned the tables with her somber tone, "I'm being serious. I don't see how you are ever going to meet anyone while you are in that profession."

"By 'anyone' do you mean an Eligible man?"

"You know exactly what I mean. What's wrong with wanting someone to settle down with or to grow old with?"

Nattie could feel the muscles on the back of her neck tightening. "There is absolutely nothing wrong with that, mother, as long as it is the right person."

Putting her mug down, Ingrid reached across the table and squeezed Nattie's hand. In her best victim tone of voice, she added, "I just want you to be happy."

With her hand on top of her mother's, Nattie attempted to reassure her mother, "I am happy."

"I know you are. But what about companionship?"

"If it happens it happens. If it doesn't it doesn't. I don't see any value in worrying about it."

Ingrid withdrew her hand and shifted to her teacher voice. "I just don't want you to worry."

"What do you want, Mother? Should I quit my job? Go back to school? Put an ad in the paper?"

Ingrid selected sarcastic indignation as her tone of voice this time. "Of course that's what I want; quit your job, put an ad in the paper, and go back to school. I hear belly dancers are making a comeback."

Wow, sarcasm. That's something new in your bag of tricks.

"Can you just answer one question for me?"

"Yes, Mother, what is it?"

Standing up, Ingrid placed a hand on Nattie's shoulder. "Are you still in love with Nathan?"

Their eyes locked for a long moment. "Yes."

Ingrid's hand closed into a squeeze. "Then please, honey, don't just take the 'if it happens it happens' attitude. If you want him, take him; you know he's yours." A smile and another squeeze marked the end of the conversation. "I'm going to the little girl's room."

Loving him and wanting him are not the same thing. It takes a lot more than that to make a marriage work, lamented Nattie.

While her mother was otherwise occupied Nattie took a bottle of Shiraz from her backpack and poured four glugs into the soup pot. Before marrying Lionel, Ingrid would not have thought twice about cooking with wine; but Lionel did not allow alcohol in the house so Nattie had to improvise. The recipe called for a cup of wine and, according to Delia, a glug was approximately a quarter cup.

Nattie had the wine stowed away before her mother returned. "My turn, and then I have to go." I have to go and then I have to go passed through her thoughts, which led her to the next thought, Oh great! Now I'm thinking like Kevin.

12

"Do you have an appointment?" asked Ingrid as she walked arm in arm with Nattie to the front door.

"I do. It's a case that I haven't decided I'm going to take yet."

"What about lunch?"

"I'll grab a bite where I'm going."

"Where is that?"

"Why the questions, Mom?" She looked more closely at her mother. "You already know where I'm going, don't you?"

Ingrid tried unsuccessfully to fight off her smug smile.

Nattie pointed an accusatory finger. "Kevin told you I'm having lunch at Nathan's place." I'll kill him.

"As long as you are there, you might as well make the most of it."

"Look, Mom, I appreciate your concern, I really do; but things with Nathan are complicated."

Ingrid laid her hands on Nattie's shoulders. "Too complicated for Natasha McMoreland? I don't think so. You, my darling daughter," she added, kissing Nattie's forehead lightly, "can do whatever you put your mind to."

Nattie noticed that her mother had mispronounced McMorales but let it go. "Thanks, Mom. You do OK for yourself too."

Ingrid smiled and whispered, "I'll let you in on a secret. While you were in the bathroom, I put a cup of Merlot in the soup."

CHAPTER 3

CONFRONTING NATHAN
(Saturday, early afternoon)

Nattie lunged for her water glass. She had eaten the Our House chili before. Our House, Nathan's tavern, was known for two things: the first was that every hour on the hour the patrons would sing "Our House" by Crosby, Stills, and Nash; and the other was a menu that featured several variations of hamburger, all loaded and all cheap. Chili was usually the healthiest thing on the menu, but this was not the same chili. This chili was flaming hot.

"What did you do to the chili?"

"What do you mean?" Nathan asked with an innocence that had never fooled her when they were married. It was certainly not going to fool her now.

Gulping down half a beer stein of water, Nattie ignored his question. "Boo?" she asked.

"Boo." He nodded. "Do you like it?"

She looked at the bowl on the bar in front of her, "Well, it should increase your beer sales."

"Do you want a beer then?"

"No thanks, but I am going to need more crackers."

"Crackers are free," he complained.

"Not my fault."

Nathan smiled and then reached under the bar to retrieve a basket full of saltine cracker packets. "Anything else?" he asked, leaning forward to watch her crumble several crackers into her chili bowl.

She held up a finger as she took another small spoon full.

"Hey, Nathan, how's it going?" called out a male voice passing behind Nattie.

"Hey, Buddy," Nathan answered, relying on the name he used when he did not know the name. "I'm hanging in there. How's it going with you?"

"OK," the newcomer answered as he sat at the bar. "I called an order in."

"Two bacon cheeseburgers?"

The newcomer nodded yes, "Say what's with that Jeep outside?"

"The four-door Jeep?"

"Yeah, with the botched paint job."

Putting a white paper bag on the bar, Nathan laughed, "That's not a botched paint job. It's Mango."

The customer handed over twelve dollars. "Really? I thought someone was trying for University of Tennessee orange." Walking out he added, "I still think it's a mistake."

Returning to Nattie, Nathan explained, "It's Boo's Jeep. I think it's a mistake too. Is the chili better?" he asked while her mouth was still full.

"Much," she said after swallowing. "It also helps that I was prepared for it this time."

"Maybe I should put a warning label on the bowl. I don't want anyone to get hurt in here."

"It's funny you should mention people getting hurt, Nathan."

She had waited for a natural time to broach the subject of Frank Lester and had been very careful to use a conversational tone, but the effort was to no avail. Nathan, ever vigilant as to her disapproval stiffened immediately and stepped back.

"What?" he asked in a lower voice.

"We need to talk about that guy who threatened you last week."

Nathan squinted and began pacing back and forth. "It was no big deal, Nattie, really. Just a misunderstanding. Nothing more."

Nattie raised an eyebrow. "And yet, shortly after threatening you he was attacked in his own driveway."

Nathan stopped his pacing, leaned back against the bar, and relaxed his shoulders. "Do you really think that was me? Come on, Nattie. Can you picture me doing something like that?"

"No. I don't think you did it, Nathan."

He grinned, "You see, no problem."

"The problem, Nate, is that you are a person of interest."

"But you know I didn't do it."

She leaned closer. "I know you couldn't have done it, but the police don't know you like I do."

Nathan bowed his head and began to trace his index finger lightly over the back of Nattie's hand. "No one knows me like you do, Nattie."

Nattie watched him for several moments before slowly raising her head. "Does Randi Lester know you, Nathan?" Her voice was matter-of-fact.

The question startled him enough that he gasped and quickly jerked his head back. Nattie regretted the harshness of her question.

"I told you I was seeing someone months ago, Nattie. Don't you remember when we drove back from that tavern out in Barton Square? You went there to interview Boo, remember?"

His tentative eye contact and nervous glances reminded her of a hamster. She watched him silently.

"I know," he confessed in a lower voice. "I didn't mention that she was married." He spread his arms. "Can you blame me?"

To this question she added a raised eyebrow to her silence.

Nathan blushed. "I guess that was a silly question. Blaming your ex-husband is the national pastime for ex-wives."

Ex-wives with nothing better to do, maybe, thought Nattie. Out loud, however, she sought to reassure him. "Look, Nathan, I am not here to blame you; but I am going to need to talk to you about her."

"I don't see why," he stated curtly. "It was just a fling. Someone to spend some time with and that's about all it was. And now it's over, so case closed."

Nattie's eyes narrowed. "And yet her husband came here and threatened you."

He took his turn to be silent.

"Did your relationship with her end before or after he threatened you?" If it ended at all.

"Before," he stated indignantly. "It isn't really any of your business though, is it? It's not like I'm your client."

"No, I am," came the deep resounding voice of Boo Robinette. Neither had noticed him enter from the kitchen.

Nathan turned and pointed at the big man. "You are?" He paused. "You are what? Her client?"

Boo nodded. "I hired her. She's going to find out who really took a baseball bat to that guy who came in here to threaten you."

Nathan looked confused. "That was before you started working here, wasn't it?"

"I was here that night," Boo remembered. "I sat right there where she is now."

Nathan snapped his fingers. "You were drinking Southern Comfort and tonic."

Boo nodded.

Leaning on the bar with his left elbow and with his back to Nattie, Nathan effectively cut her out of the conversation. "Why do you think I need a detective? According to the police I'm just a, a— What did they call it?"

"A person of interest," Nattie offered from over his shoulder.

Nathan stepped back to include her once again. "And that's not so bad, right, Nattie?"

Nattie cocked her head. "It's not much evidence. Still, people have been convicted on pretty shaky evidence in the past."

"I'm not concerned about the police. I doubt they really think you did it anyway," explained Boo. "I'm worried about that nut job. Until we figure out who really did it, he's going to blame you and that means he is going to be coming back. Somewhere, sometime, he is going to be evening the score. I could see it in his eyes."

Nathan dismissed Boo's concern with a flip of his hand. "He's not coming back. He doesn't care about her that much."

"That doesn't matter to guys like him."

17

"What does matter to guys like him, Boo?" asked Nattie in a teacher-like tone that told Nathan the question was for his benefit.

Addressing Nattie but speaking to Nate, Boo explained, "To understand guys like him you have to recognize that they are wired differently than everyone else. To you, if there is a problem your first instinct is to negotiate. While you are thinking about a peaceful solution a guy like him will view it as hesitation and go right for a quick solution regardless of how much violence it takes. Normal people are just not equipped to match that kind of thinking. If threatened they are particularly dangerous, and to him, Nate here took something that belongs to him. That's a threat. It doesn't matter if he wants her or not. To him, she is a belonging and Nate is a thief. Scaring Nate might have been enough for him then, but that was before someone broke his leg with a baseball bat." Boo turned to face Nate squarely. "He is not going to let that go."

"Which means he now thinks he has two scores to settle with you," added Nattie, repeating Boo's words.

Nathan glared at her but said nothing. There was nothing to say. She was right about this. She knew things about him and Randi that he did not want her to know, and she was right about that too. She was always right and he resented her for it. *Why can't she just be a little bit more human?* he wondered for the umpteenth time.

"OK," he said turning toward Boo. "I agree I need help. But why her?"

Yeah, Nattie thought, why me?

CHAPTER 4

NATTIE VISITS FRANK LESTER
(late Saturday afternoon)

Nattie could have found Frank Lester's hospital room without looking at the numbers over the doors. It was the room where all the laughter was coming from. As she neared the nurses' station, two nurses walked out of the room, their heads together, still laughing.

"Can you believe the chutzpah of that guy?"

"I thought Dr. Hester was going to swallow her face when he asked her for a sponge bath."

More laughter. "I have never seen anyone talk to her like that, have you?"

The other nurse shook her head emphatically. "Are you kidding me? Her? I just saw it and I still don't believe it."

"Did you see her face when he first asked?"

"No, I had my back to her at that point."

"Well let me tell you. Her first reaction was exactly what you would have expected." She paused. "There was castration in her eyes."

"I'm sure."

"But then he just sort of grinned at her."

"Grinned?"

"Yeah, grinned. He transformed his face from marine to little boy. Really, he looked like a little boy who just got caught feeding his green beans to the dog."

"Is that when she laughed?"

"It is."

"That's when I turned around. I've never heard her laugh before."

They had still not seen Nattie at the desk, but looked back down the hall. "Is she still in there?"

"I guess so." More snickering. "Don't suppose he's getting his sponge bath, do you?"

They jumped in unison as Nattie cleared her throat. "Could you help me? I'm trying to find a patient's room."

They looked embarrassed but quickly regained their composure. The one farthest from Nattie lowered her eyes and circled the desk, leaving the other nurse to tend to the visitor. "What's the name?"

"Lester. Frank Lester."

Red washed over the nurse's face. "I am dreadfully sorry. We were—" She fumbled for the words.

"We were being catty," chimed in the other.

"We meant no disrespect for your—"

Nattie waved her hand. "Please don't worry. This is a professional visit. I've never meet Mr. Lester before."

The nurse sighed in relief.

Nattie waited but had to remind her of the question. "The room?"

Slapping her forehead, the nurse pointed down the hall. "Third door on the left."

"Thank you." Then, after taking two steps toward the room, Nattie turned back. Both nurses were behind the desk watching her. "Do you think they're done by now?" She walked down the hall to the wonderful sound of spontaneous laughter.

A thin, dark-haired woman in a white doctor's coat walked briskly from the room, nearly colliding with Nattie just as she got to it. Dr. Hester had one of those faces that could have been attractive if she smiled; but the angular features were only sharpened by her stern expression. The high collar, buttoned up to her chin, didn't help matters. This woman could play the lead in *Wicked* without a costume.

"Excuse me." The doctor, startled, stepped backward.

"No harm. Is that Frank Lester's room?"

Dr. Hester nodded. "Are you his wife?" Then, when Nattie shook her head, she asked, "Are you another sister?"

Before Nattie had to lie about who she was, the doctor's pager called her away, "That's his room. His sister is in there with him now. Please excuse me." Without waiting for a reply, she circled Nattie and continued down the hall with short, choppy steps. Her head she kept perfectly even, but the tightly bound ponytail bounced from side to side.

Stepping into the doorway of the room, Nattie raised her hand to knock and announce her presence; but the scene before her was too intriguing to disturb right away. The patient's right leg was enveloped in a huge cast suspended by a weighted pulley and cable attached to a frame at the end of the bed. The woman Dr. Hester had taken to be Frank Lester's sister was leaning over the bed. Her right wrist was in the grip of his left hand and he was pulling her over. With his right hand he was trying to pull her shirt up.

"Stop it!" she said through clinched teeth as she swatted at his arm with her free hand.

This was Nattie's cue to knock, startling both of them. The man in the bed dropped his right hand away, but kept hold of her wrist. From that awkward position she was able straighten her shirt. All the while he kept his eyes on Nattie without altering the silly grin on his face.

"My name is Natasha McMorales." Even as she spoke the words, Nattie wondered why she did not use her real name. "Are you Frank Lester?"

"He is," answered the woman while she wrested her hand free and stepped away from the bed.

"I am doing a follow-up investigation on the attack on you. Would this be a good time for me to ask you a few questions?"

"I was just leaving," said the woman. "He's all yours." With that she took a sweater from the back of a chair, placed it over her arm, and made for the door.

"Are you with the police?" asked Frank.

"No, I am a private investigator out of Bristol."

21

"Of course you are. Where else would a detective named Natasha McMuffin be from?"

Rolling her eyes and taking a slow deep breath, Nattie corrected him. "That's Natasha McMorales and it is an agency name. My name is Nattie Moreland and the Natasha McMorales Agency is mine."

Hearing Nattie's real name stopped the woman in the doorway. She turned and eyed the detective for a moment. At five ten or so, she stood half a head taller than Nattie. Dark hair, alabaster skin, and crystal clear blue eyes accented her dark red lips. Her figure, chunky by today's standards, would have been called voluptuous during Marilyn Monroe's day. The deep neckline meant that voluptuous was what she was aiming at as well.

"I don't remember hiring a private eye. Did you hire a private eye?"

"No," said the woman in the doorway, who then turned and left.

"So who is picking up your tab?"

"My client is not really important. What is more important is that I—"

Frank interrupted her. "It is important to me."

"Well, Mr. Lester, I do not have permission to reveal my client. If it is important to you, I can see about getting permission."

"It is important to me," he said with a smile.

"But since I am here, can I go ahead and ask a few questions? My interest is simply to find out who attacked you. Surely that is something you would want to cooperate with."

"You would think so." Frank was still smiling politely.

Hoping a direct question might trip him up, she asked, "Do you know who attacked you?"

"How would I? I was attacked from behind."

"That is my understanding, but you might still know who did it."

"Don't you think I would have told the police investigator if I knew who it was?"

"Would you?"

His grin got bigger. "So you don't know, do you?"

"What's that, Mr. Lester?"

"You don't know what I have already told the police, do you?"

"I have not gotten the police report yet, but rest assured that I will be coordinating my efforts with the official police investigation."

Frank laughed. "I am sure you will, missy, but don't you think it strange that you didn't start there? I mean, it makes me wonder who you are working for and what you are doing here."

"I will have that information for you tomorrow, Mr. Lester."

"Well then, why don't you come back tomorrow?"

"OK, then, I will say good night and wish you a swift recovery."

As Nattie turned to go, Frank called out, "You don't have to leave, do you?"

"I hardly see a reason to stay, Mr. Lester."

"Oh, I have a good reason for you to stay."

She waited for him to explain; but when he just grinned at her she asked, "What is that?"

"You can help me with the bed pan."

I could be persuaded to help you wear it after you fill it, she thought. "I'll pass, but I will send a nurse."

As she entered the hall, he shouted after her, "Give my best to Nathan when you see him."

CHAPTER 5

RANDI LESTER

"Please wait."

It was an unfamiliar voice that called out from behind her when Nattie reached the front door, but the two benches in the hallway that passed for a lobby were empty so she knew the request was meant for her. Stopping and turning slowly to her right, Nattie met the eyes of the woman from Frank Lester's room. She was approaching from the hallway marked "Café/Gift Shop," a waxed paper cup with a straw in her right hand.

"Do you know who I am?" she asked as she neared Nattie.

"I assume you are Randi Lester."

"That's right. And you are Nathan's ex-wife."

Wow, Nattie thought, you get right to it don't you? I bet you are more coy when it's a man in your sights. "I am Nathan's ex-wife. I was not all that sure that you would know who I was."

Randi arched her right eyebrow slightly. "I have to admit, you don't look like I pictured you, but I know you. I'm the one who recommended that Beau call you to protect Nathan."

"You are?" Nattie voice expressed surprise.

"Yes."

"Why me?"

"Nathan brags about you. If you are half as good as he says you are, then that's one good reason." She hesitated. "I suppose that is why I pictured you as more—" She struggled for the right word.

"Statuesque?" guessed Nattie.

Randi didn't reply.

Nattie fought off the temptation to look at Randi's chest.

"I thought you'd be more of an Amazon." Randi blurted the words out.

Nattie spread her hands. "Nope, this is me, shrimp that I am."

No response.

"Was there another reason for calling me?"

Randi looked at her like the answer was obvious. "I just think that you will be quite a bit more motivated with Nathan in danger."

Nattie weighed her response before asking, "How much danger would you say Nathan is in?"

"Don't let Frank's playfulness fool you. He thinks Nathan broke his leg, and that is not good for Nathan."

"So you know Mr. Robinette too?" *That means you are still connected to Nathan.*

Randi handed Nattie a slip of paper with a phone number on it. "I do, but that is another story. I just wanted to catch you and say that I am willing to do whatever I can do to help."

Nattie looked at the paper. "Thank you."

"I didn't want any awkwardness between us to get in the way of solving this."

Feigning ignorance, Nattie repeated, "Awkwardness?"

Lowering her eyebrows now, Randi quietly replied, "Look, Ms. Moreland, I know you think I'm some kind of tramp, and maybe you are justified, but don't treat me like I'm stupid."

Good for you, Randi. "Fair enough, Ms Lester."

"Randi, please."

"Fair enough, Randi. I am sure I will want to ask you some questions eventually, but right now I am not that far along. Is there anything you think I should know?"

"The first thing I want you to know is that Nathan could not have done this."

Nattie eyed her closely. "Are you his alibi?"

"No, I was home when it happened. I just know Nathan could not have done this."

"I know that too." It surprised her how much she was bothered by Randi's presumption that she could give some insight into the character of her ex-husband.

Randi reached out and rested her fingertips on Nattie's left forearm, "I'm sorry. Of course you know Nathan could not have done this. I felt it needed to be said."

"Thank you," Nattie found herself saying without thinking.

Randi smiled warmly for a brief moment and then the smile faded as her eyes shifted toward the front entrance.

Nattie turned to see a man walking from the parking garage. He was six feet tall, of average weight, and casually dressed.

"That's Henry Quayle. He's the investigator. He is going to want to talk to you."

Nattie turned back to face Randi.

"Do you know where Starbucks is?" Randi asked.

"The coffee shop by exit seven?"

Randi nodded.

"Can you meet me there at nine o'clock?"

"Sure."

"Good." Randi nodded again, "I will see you then. Good luck with Henry."

The parting comment was confusing, "What does that mean?"

Randi looked toward Henry, who was still on the sidewalk and then back at Nattie. "You are about to meet Henry." With that she smiled and went out to where Henry stood.

Nattie watched as Henry put his hands in his windbreaker pockets and began to speak. Randi gestured at her watch, shrugged, and pointed at Nattie. Henry Quayle studied Nattie for a long moment, then turned to say something to Randi, who nodded. He bowed his head and began making his way to Nattie. Over his shoulder Nattie watched as Randi mouthed the word "sorry" and hurried off.

CHAPTER 6

HENRY QUAYLE

Henry Quayle did not look to the right or to the left as he approached Nattie. He simply stared directly at her, walking at her in the same manner. His expression was nondescript: not pleasant, not angry, not even suspicious.

Nattie tried to coax a smile from him with one of her own, but he showed no sign of recognition.

"I have been told that you are a private investigator," he said as he got close enough to be heard but while still too far to be discreet. "Is that true?"

"It is." Nattie passed him a business card. "I'm Natalie Moreland. I'm glad to meet you. I understand you are in charge of the investigation into the attack on Frank Lester."

"That is correct," he told her without looking up from her business card.

Did I misspell something on my business card, wondered Nattie as she looked at him looking at it.

Henry looked up at her. "I am a bit of an anthropologist. With your fair skin and blonde hair I would have said you were of Anglo-Saxon descent when I first saw you. It just goes to show what a melting pot the world is becoming. Natasha is more Central European, isn't it? Maybe Eastern European? Is it a family name?"

Embarrassed that her new business cards did not eliminate the confusion, Nattie stammered, "Actually Natasha is not my name. That is the name of the agency." *I already told you once.* "I am Natalie Moreland."

"Of course," Henry continued, "the name Natasha is not as common in Eastern Europe as most Americans think. Most of us first heard that name on the Rocky and Bullwinkle cartoon show. That is the mind for you; once an idea takes root in there it is difficult to get it out."

I can see that.

"But the name McMorales is certainly more Western European."

"Actually, it is a made-up name."

"Oh, I am sure of that. Probably by a relative when entering the country. If I had to guess, I would say that your family name was Morales and your people came here through Boston."

Nattie attempted to placate the investigator, who seemed determined to pursue his speculations. "So you would guess that they added the 'Mc' in order to fit in better?"

Henry nodded. "That happened much more often than you think. Records of immigrants en route were not kept, of course, so we don't know what the names were before they registered." Pausing and looking up and to the left gave the impression of deep consideration about what was next to be said, "I'd say that before the Civil War 26 or 27 percent of immigrants changed their family names."

Smiling politely, Nattie thought, *Do you seriously expect that making up specific statistics makes you more credible?*

"That is just an educated guess, mind you, but it is probably accurate within a few percentage points."

"Like I said, Mr. Quayle—it is Mr. Quayle, isn't it? Mrs. Lester gave me your name before she left."

"Henry. Henry Quayle."

"Good to meet you, Mr. Quayle. And you are the detective on the Frank Lester case, right?"

"Quayle is an Anglo-Saxon name, but look at me; I look less Anglo than you."

"Like I said, that is not my name."

"Moreland, is it?"

28

So you knew all along. "Yes, Moreland."

"Well, Ms. Moreland, you are very lucky that it is me on this case."

Lucky is not the word that comes to my mind. "How so?"

"Most real detectives would resent a private investigator getting involved with one of their cases."

Real detectives?

"I suppose they figure that a private investigator will either get in the way or show them up." He laughed. "One is just as bad as the other to some of them." He stopped laughing when he noticed that Nattie did not find it as amusing as he did. "I am not so territorial as others. I am perfectly willing to keep the lines of communication open with a private investigator."

Oh course you are. Who else are you going to talk to? "I am delighted to hear that, Real Detective Quayle. I am looking forward to getting this solved. And I can assure you that if I happen to discover who attacked Frank Lester first I will let you know immediately."

Waving his hand in dismissal, "Oh, I already know who did it. I don't have all the proof yet, but I know exactly who it was." Furrowing his brow and leaning forward, he added, "He's done it before."

Startled into speechlessness until she swallowed hard, "Who?"

"That was good. For a moment there I thought you were going to say 'whom,' but you said it correctly."

"You say you already know who it was."

"Indeed. In fact, I know why."

Nattie waited.

"I suppose you want to know."

"It would certainly speed up my investigation," Nattie took her turn to laugh, but quickly realized that the detective found her as amusing as she had found him. "Yes, please."

"I can tell you that it is someone well known to us."

"Does this person have a name?" *And could you just give it to me without torturous speculations of his family's origins?*

"He does indeed, but I am not at liberty to give it to you at this time. You see, the investigation of his earlier attack was never closed. It was suspended. The decision to reopen it is not mine to make. Schneider, Douglas Schneider, was the original detective; and it will have to be his decision, not mine, to give you the name."

29

Nattie wrote the name down on the small notebook she kept in her pocket. "I'll be getting in touch with Detective Schneider, then."

"I think it will be better if you let me set that up for you."

"Why is that, Detective Quayle?"

"It's tricky. Cops are more finicky when it comes to investigating one of their own."

"What are you saying? Frank Lester was attacked by a...cop?"

He nodded. "A former cop."

CHAPTER 7

KEVIN'S BATTERY

Nattie looked at her watch as she buckled into her Subaru. It was 6:30 and she had not eaten anything since Boo's chili at the Our House Tavern. With two and a half hours to kill before her meeting with Randi, she would normally go somewhere for something to eat. Abingdon was full of places she liked, but nothing sounded good to her. *Maybe I'm not hungry*, she thought, and then laughed at the absurdity.

A Magnificent Seven breakfast at Perkins was what she wanted. Hunger was not part of the formula. Having breakfast at night was "cozy," and she was in the mood for cozy. Plus, with free refills and a copy of John McDonald's new book, *In His Right Mind*, in her bag, she could easily kill a couple of hours and be ready for her nine o'clock meeting.

Twenty minutes later, as she reached for the front door at Perkins, her phone rang.

"Kevin?" she asked, knowing it was him.

"Hey, Sarge. What are you doing?"

"I'm about to go into Perkins. Why?"

"Do you still have jumper cables in your trunk?"

Great. "I do." She waited for him to ask.

He waited for her to ask. When she said nothing, he continued, "My lights were left on and my battery is dead."

"Kevin?"

"Yes."

"Didn't I give you a car emergency kit for Christmas?"

"You did."

"Isn't there a set of jumper cables in there?"

"Oh yeah, there probably is."

"Well?"

"Well," he repeated. "The only thing is—"

"It's not in the car, is it?"

No answer.

"Why isn't it in your car, Kevin?"

"I don't know. I just haven't gotten around to it. Can you come help me?"

I could but I'm not going to. "Where are you?"

"I'm at the Racket Club. Do you know where that is?"

Slinging her bag onto the passenger seat, she answered, "I do. I'll be there in twenty minutes. And, Kevin?"

"Yes."

"You carried that emergency kit out of Mom's house when you left, right?"

"Yeah."

"Where did you go?"

"I drove home."

"So you took the kit from mom's house to your car, right?"

"Yeah."

"And then you drove home, right?"

"Yeah."

"And when you got home you took it inside, right?"

"Of course. Where are you going with this?"

Is it me or could he be this thick? "It was in your car, Kevin. Why didn't you just leave it in your car?"

An exasperated sigh issued from the other end of the phone. "I took all my presents inside. I always keep gifts right next to my desk until I write thank you cards for them. How do you do it?"

Nattie looked at herself in the rearview mirror. *It is you.* "I'll see you in twenty minutes."

"Thanks sis."

The hood of Kevin's beat-up old Mustang was open. A Honda Civic with its hood open was parked directly in front of it. As Nattie got closer, Kevin and a girl got out of the Civic.

Unlike Kevin, who was dressed in jeans, the girl wore tennis tights and what looked like brand new cross-trainers.

"This is Angela."

"Hi," she said. *She couldn't be more than seventeen.*

"I'm Kevin's sister, Nattie."

Angela smiled. "Kevin says you are a CIA agent."

Nattie's eyes narrowed. "Did he now?"

"I said she works for the agency, not the Central Intelligence Agency," Kevin explained. He returned Nattie's glare. "Although she could run the CIA if she wanted."

"I have a private investigation agency," she explained to Angela.

Angela smiled sweetly. *The look of embarrassment in her eyes could have been for her own misunderstanding or it could have been for Kevin's big fish story being exposed. Either way, she is too young for you, Kevin.*

Nattie opened the trunk; and while Kevin rooted around for her jumper cables, he said, "Angela will give me a jump."

Angela was looking in the other direction and did not appear to have heard his remark.

Leaning closer to him, Nattie whispered, "You had better mean jump your car, Kevin."

Kevin laughed. "Come on, Nattie. I just met her. She was in my tennis class. Who do you think I am?"

Nattie looked at him, *You are no Romeo.* Then she looked at the girl in the tennis tights, *but you are a guy.* She moved stand next to Angela while Kevin attached the cables. "So, what kind of tennis player is my brother?"

Angela chuckled. "I'm not sure what kind of tennis player he's going to be, but he's going to be fun to have in class."

That figures.

Between giggles, Angela added. "Do you want to hear what he asked the pro?"

Nattie offered her a resigned nod.

"The first time he hit a ball into the net he asked when the kids were going to show up to retrieve balls." More giggling. "He thought there would be ball boys."

That's my brother. "It was very nice of you to help him out. I hope you didn't miss anything."

"Oh no, I'm fine. I had to wait for my boyfriend anyway. He works the front desk."

Nattie smiled.

CHAPTER 8

PERKINS

Arriving at Starbucks early, she again took *In His Right Mind* from her bag and started across the parking lot.

"Nattie!" called Randi from the open window of a Jeep Cherokee. "I know this was my idea, but I haven't eaten all day. Could we go somewhere to get something more substantial?"

"Of course. Where would you like to go?"

"Perkins, if that is OK with you."

Ten minutes later they were settling into a booth and ordering decaf coffee.

"Do you know what you want?" asked the waitress.

"I do," answered Randi, "but she will need another minute."

"Actually, I'm ready too. Go ahead."

"I'd like the Mag Seven, please. With bacon and make my eggs over easy. I know it's weird, but sometimes I just crave breakfast for dinner."

"I'll have the same, but scramble my eggs."

After the waitress left, they looked awkwardly at each other.

Nattie broke the silence. "Breakfast for dinner is not weird to me. In my family we had a breakfast dinner whenever it was late. And when we were traveling, and we always got home late."

The breakfast/family small talk did not bring a response from Randi so Nattie continued, "What do you think I need to know?"

Randi opened her mouth, but caught her words as the waitress returned with their coffees. While Nattie opened a Splenda packet for hers, Randi took a sip from her mug.

"I suppose the most important thing I wanted to say is what I have already said. I don't believe Nathan attacked Frank." Pausing to look directly across the table at Nattie, "You don't think he did it either, do you?"

"Direct confrontation is not Nathan's style." *But I don't know what he might do if a well-endowed damsel in distress stroked his ego.*

"The second most important thing for you to know is that no matter what Frank says, he believes Nathan did it and intends to get even." Randi punctuated her statement with a tip of her head. "That's the most important thing—that this is serious."

"I can assure you, Mrs. Lester, that I would not have taken the case unless I was prepared to take it seriously."

Randi squinted at the reference to her marital status. "I really don't expect us to be friends—"

You got that right.

"—but I would really prefer that you call me Randi. I'm not planning on being Mrs. Lester for much longer."

A wave of thoughts and questions flooded Nattie's mind immediately. Don't go there, she told herself.

She did not have to fight off her imagination for long because their breakfasts arrived. Neither woman spoke as they prepped their dinners with salt, pepper, butter, and syrup. Perkins had the best pancakes in town, at least according to Nattie, but tonight she barely noticed their taste at all.

With her first bite of pancakes still on her fork, Randi said, "I also wanted to clear the air. Nathan and I have seen each other socially—"

Socially. Is that what you call it? Socially.

"—as I am sure you know. That is the second reason I wanted to talk to you."

36

"To tell me that you know that I know that you and Nathan have been together?"

Randi's forehead furrowed as she deciphered Nattie's sentence. "I wanted to get past any awkwardness between us because I don't want you to hesitate to ask me anything you think will help you find out who really attacked Frank."

"I appreciate your—" Finding the right word was a struggle. Nattie finally hit on "straightforwardness." She congratulated herself for finishing the sentence. "I, of course, have one big question."

"Good. Go ahead and ask me anything you want about Nathan and me, or Frank and me—anything you want, anything at all."

"Do you have any idea of who attacked Frank?"

The question caused Randi to jerk slightly and to raise her eyebrows. "I don't know why I didn't expect that question." Her face broke out into a grin. "Of course you would ask me that. Sometimes I'm such a ditz."

Women who look like you can make a whole career out of ditziness.

"No. I can't think of anyone in particular who might have done this. But it doesn't surprise me that someone did it. Frank is a bully. He gets off on intimidating people." She spread her arms. "It would not surprise me if he mixed it up with someone on the way home from the store and got followed home."

"Let's hope that's not what happened. It would be hard to find who did it if the attack were that spontaneous. Is there anyone you can think of who might have had a score to settle with Frank?"

Randi held a finger up while she finished her bite of eggs before answering the question. "I don't know of anyone in particular. Frank did not include me in any of his business dealings, but I heard the way he talked to people on the phone. I saw how he treated strangers. He could be charming when he wanted to be; but if something didn't go his way, he could get very rude and very insulting very fast. And if he thought he was being challenged or disrespected, then this whole other angry person would come out."

"So he made enemies."

Randi rolled her eyes. "Everyone he ever knew or dealt with is a potential enemy. He doesn't treat anyone nice."

"Including you?" Nattie voiced the question before she could stop herself.

Randi, who had been making steady progress on her breakfast while they talked, put her fork down and gazed at Nattie. "Including me." She lowered her voice. "Have you heard of battered woman's syndrome?"

"I've heard of it, but explain it to me."

"You don't even realize you are being abused. It happens gradually, and before you know it you are isolated, dependent, and numb."

Nattie put her fork down, folded her hands, and rested her arms on the edge of the table. "Are you being battered?"

"Emotionally," Randi answered calmly. "My therapist says that Frank is abusing me emotionally. He pinches me around the waist when he thinks I'm putting on weight, and he can be a little rough when we are being intimate; but he never hits me. Hitting a woman is beneath him. Controlling, criticizing, belittling, embarrassing, and calling me names are OK, though." She said all this with the same display of emotion she would have shown had they been talking about the weather. Breaking eye contact, she concentrated on her food.

Nattie waited.

Randi ate the last of her eggs and another bite of her pancakes before picking up her coffee as a sign she had finished. More than half her pancakes remained on her plate. "I never realized what was happening. I thought I was just having trouble sleeping. A friend suggested I go see a therapist."

Nattie pushed her plate to the edge of the table with several bites of pancake left on it. *It's not succumbing to peer pressure if I eat a lot more than she did. I just don't want her to think I ate everything.* "Is it helping?"

"What?"

"Is the therapy helping you sleep?"

Randi chuckled. "I was going to say it is helping a lot. I feel much, much better, but I haven't thought about the therapy helping me sleep for a while. I just feel more content with being me."

"Well that could make you sleep better, I would think."

"It surely has. This whole therapy thing is new to me. Have you ever gone to therapy?"

Nattie shook her head. "I wanted to be a counselor when I was in college, but that didn't work out." *I tried to get Nathan to go with me to marriage counseling, but I'm not going to share that with you.*

"If you want to know the truth, it was Nathan's idea that I go get therapy in the first place."

Really! "Really?"

"Refill?" asked the waitress.

"Yes, please." Randi extended her cup.

Really?

"Ma'am?"

Therapy was Nathan's idea?

"Would you like more coffee, ma'am?"

"I'm sorry," Nattie said with a start, "I must have been daydreaming." She had to look around the table for her cup. "Yes, please."

"Are you OK?" asked Randi when the waitress left with their dishes.

Not really. "Oh yes, I think I was just having a senior moment. What were you saying about Nathan?"

"Do you want the long story or the short story?"

Nattie shrugged. "I've got nowhere else to be and the refills are free here, so give me the long version."

"Well it's the story of how I met Nathan. I figured you would need to hear about it; but I wasn't sure if it might bother you, seeing how you two were married. But Nathan said you were way over him."

Nattie smiled weakly. Nathan doesn't have a clue.

"So you're fine to hear about it?"

"Absolutely."

"I guess it started with Frank being gone. He is a helicopter pilot and he was doing his second tour of duty—in Afghanistan. His first was in Iraq. Anyway, I was alone, which does not usually bother me. I'm not a normal woman. I guess I've always been a loner. I never really had girlfriends to talk to or hang out with. I never went in for girl talk."

You sure seem chatty now.

"I think being in therapy has taught me the value of talking. You know, you remind me a little of my therapist. You don't really look like Charlotte, but you watch me when I talk like she does. It's like I can see it in your eyes that you are listening to me."

"Charlotte Stevens?"

"Yes, that's her. Do you know her?"

"I've never met her myself, but she was very helpful to a friend of mine whose husband was murdered not too long ago. Do you like her?"

"I do, very much."

"And she has helped you open up?"

Randi held her coffee cup up as a salute. "And sleep too."

Nattie raised her cup and tapped Randi's. "To Charlotte."

After a drink from her cup, Randi continued, "Anyway, with Frank overseas I started having a hard time sleeping. My life was just going to work and doing aerobic workouts at home. After a while I started going out to bars late. That was better than going stir crazy at home alone."

"But you live outside of Abingdon, don't you?"

"Washington County."

"Well the Our House is downtown Bristol. Why go that far from home?"

"I tried a couple of places out at Exit Seven, but there were too many guys wanting to hook up. I was looking for a place to kill an hour or two without being hassled."

"And the Our House fit the bill?"

"It did. I'd go in about eleven o'clock or so and stay until closing."

"Every night?"

"Not in the beginning, but it got to be most nights pretty quick."

"And you and Nathan hit it off."

"At first he never said anything to me other than 'what will you have' or 'do you want another?'"

But I guarantee he noticed you.

"Then one night a couple of guys sat down on either side of me and started talking to each other about me."

"What were they saying?"

"Just the usual guy-in-a-bar-trying-to-hit-on-a-girl stuff."

How would I know what that is?

"Nathan told them that I wanted to be left alone, so they went away. I thanked him and that's when we first really spoke."

Nattie pointed at her finger. "Were you wearing your ring?"

Randi stared at her wedding ring. "I was."

So Nathan knew you were married.

"But we didn't date or anything then."

Or anything?

"Nathan and I did not date until Frank and I were separated, and that didn't happen until I realized that he was emotionally abusive."

"But you weren't divorced yet?"

"No," she answered meekly, "I wasn't. I'm not proud of that, but I think I needed to believe I had someone waiting for me when it was over with Frank." Her head and shoulders drooped and she sighed. "I haven't been single since I was in junior high school. Charlotte says my dependence on men is because I never got what I needed from my father."

Curious, thought Nattie, *I bet she would say my independence from men is because of my father. The alcoholic.*

"He raised me by himself from when I was twelve on. He probably did the best that he could, but he was an alcoholic who couldn't take care of himself, much less me."

Nattie held her gaze.

Randi looked away for a moment and slowly looked back. "I know that's no excuse, but that's the best I could do at the time."

"You were telling me about Nathan before you dated."

"Oh yes," she answered with more energy. "He encouraged me to go to a counselor because he thought I was becoming an alcoholic. He thought I was self-prescribing."

"Self-medicating," Nattie corrected.

"Yes, that's it, self-medicating. He told me a lot of alcoholics start by self-medicating."

"I think he's right." *And he should know.*

"That scared me. I did not want to end up like my father, so I made an appointment with Charlotte Stevens the next day."

"Let me warm those up for you."

Both women jumped. Neither had seen the waitress approach. Simultaneously, each woman glanced at her own coffee cup. Neither cup was empty.

As the waitress filled the cups, Nattie asked, "Are we in the way?"

"Nah, it's not busy, you're fine."

When she was out of earshot, Randi leaned forward. "We should leave a nice tip."

"I agree."

"So, where were we?"

"You made an appointment for therapy because Nathan thought you were self-medicating."

Randi knit her eyebrows while she considered what to say next.

Nattie filled the silence. "So, how is the drinking? Have you got it under control?"

"Oh, yeah. It's fine. I mean, I'm not an alcoholic. That doesn't mean I couldn't become one, but I'm not one now."

Nattie smiled.

"I don't drink instead of sleep anymore at all."

"That's good."

Randi nodded. "Now I go to sleep fine. I still have nightmares sometimes, but that's getting better too."

"Do you mind if I ask a personal question?"

"About the case?"

"No, about your therapy. I'm just curious."

"I don't mind. Go ahead and ask me anything."

"OK, if you are sure you don't mind."

"It's OK, really. Ask whatever you want."

"You originally went because you were concerned you might be self-medicating, right?"

"Yes."

"And you might have been, but it wasn't so far that you were an alcoholic yet, right?"

"Right."

"But why were you self-medicating? Was it that abused woman's thing?"

"Battered woman's syndrome? Maybe. We, I mean Charlotte and I, think I was self-medicating because I wasn't sleeping, but we aren't sure yet why I wasn't sleeping."

"I see."

"Wait a minute," said Randi with a stern look, "I think it might be because of the battered woman's syndrome. I mean, as soon as we figured out what was going on and I decided to leave Frank, I started sleeping again. Then when Frank came home, the sleep problems started again. It has to be Frank."

"That makes sense to me."

"Me too, but Charlotte isn't convinced. She says that very few psychological problems have just one cause. She says that simple explanations for complex issues are just for textbooks and the media."

"That makes sense too."

Randi raised her eyebrows and cocked her head.

"So the symptoms came back when Frank returned?"

Randi nodded.

"Are you still divorcing him?"

"He has the papers, but he didn't sign them. He's being difficult, which I should have expected. Now with his hospitalization, everything is on hold."

"And the ring?"

Fiddling with her wedding ring, Randi replied, "I'm just keeping the peace for now. Charlotte told me that the most dangerous time with an abusive man is when you are leaving him." Looking out the window, she added, "I know, I sound like a coward, but this is how I have to do it."

"I don't think you are a coward and I don't think you should worry about what anyone else thinks either."

Randi turned to face Nattie again. "Thank you. You're nice to say that."

"I meant it."

"I know that too."

"You know," Nattie's voice dropped, "my father was an alcoholic too."

"Really?"

"Yes, but not all my life. He was always a drinker, but he started self-medicating when he lost his job. My mother kicked him out. My brother and I—I have a younger brother—were raised by our mother."

"What was that like?"

Nattie looked confused.

"What was being raised by your mother like?"

Realizing that the question came from a woman raised by her father, Nattie treaded softly. "I suppose she did the best she could, but life with her was a roller coaster. She was one of those women who thought she had to have a man to take care of her."

Randi leaned on the edge of the table. "You mean she was a woman like me?"

Nattie could feel her lips compress. "I'm sorry. That was very insensitive of me."

"Don't worry about it, I know what I was like. There was probably a reason that your mother was like that."

"No doubt." Nattie leaned on the table too. "But you asked me how it was and I was telling you. We weren't really neglected, but I raised my brother while my mother did her thing. It was OK. Then she married a man who wanted to control us. We went from no parental control to extreme parental control."

"I guess no one has a perfect life."

"No one I know anyway. How about your mother?"

Sitting back, Randi looked out the window again. "My mother died when I was twelve."

"I'm sorry."

The head didn't move. "Thank you." There was a pause. "It was a car accident. My brother died then too. He had his permit and he was driving. He made a left turn into the wrong lane and hit a truck head on."

"How awful."

Randi nodded but her gaze never left the window. "I stayed with my aunt, my mother's sister, for a week while they tracked my father down. He was bartending in Richmond. They shipped me off to live with him." Turning at last to face Nattie, she flexed her jaw. "The last thing my aunt said to me was, 'If you go live with that drunk, you'll end up a whore.'"

Nattie's eyes widened.

"Nice, huh?"

"You were twelve?"

"I was twelve. And I had no choice about going to live with my father."

"I don't know what to say."

Randi smiled briefly and looked back out the window. "There isn't anything to say."

"No one should ever say anything like that to a twelve-year-old."

"No. They shouldn't. But she was right." Randi took a deep breath. "In Richmond I was the new girl. The guys were curious because I was new and I had boobs. The girls froze me out because I was new and had boobs. My father worked evenings; but even if he was home, he didn't have a clue, so I had absolutely zero, what did you call it, parental control. It's not that I need a man to take care of me. I can take care of myself. I just know my way around men. Sex was a tool," she said matter-of-factly. "I learned it from my brother."

They stared at each other.

44

"You know what I'm saying?"

Nattie nodded.

"So you can understand why I wonder how having a mother around might have made my life turn out a little different."

Randi's words hit Nattie deeply. She had never considered that women she had always thought of as teases might have been victims of circumstances. Her own mother, whose attitude toward men was a source of embarrassment to her, was at least always there.

Nattie reached across the table with both her hands. "Certainly."

Randi looked down at Nattie's palms without moving.

"This is probably one of those girl things that you missed out on; but when a sister holds her hands out like this it means she wants to hold your hand."

With trepidation Randi slowly brought her hands up from her lap and placed them on top of Nattie's. It was awkward and her hands were cold, but they were soft and her grip was childlike.

Randi stared at their hands with curiosity.

"No one has ever called me sister before."

Nattie squeezed her hands gently.

"That was nice."

Nattie smiled.

"Charlotte says I need to cultivate some friendships with other women. Maybe she is right."

"Probably."

Randi gave a last squeeze of Nattie's hands and withdrew them. Her expression was calm, contented.

"So you did have your mother until your were twelve. What was she like?"

The question caught Randi off guard. With a loud gasp, she covered her mouth quickly with both her hands. "I killed her."

"What?"

Randi looked around frantically. "She used to hold my hands, just like you did. I was thinking about her while we were sitting like that; but when you asked me that question, it all flooded back to me. Oh God help me." Her reddened eyes pleaded with Nattie. "I killed my mother." She reached out for Nattie's hands, which were still on the table, and held them tightly. "I killed my mother."

45

"Wait a minute, what do you mean you killed your mother? Were you charged? Was there a trial or something?"

"No, nothing like that, but I killed her." She pulled Nattie's hands toward herself. "I caused that accident. It's my fault."

"What did you do?"

While Randi struggling to keep breathing, her eyes pooled up with tears. "I never told anyone about my brother, but I hated him."

"That's understandable."

"But that day, the day they died, I yelled at him." The tears began to stream down her cheeks.

Nattie allowed Randi to sob openly, then, after a few moments, coaxed her to continue. "You yelled."

"My mother was already waiting in the car and he came up behind me and put his hands inside my shirt. I fought him off and he laughed at me. I threatened to tell, but he just grabbed me again and told me no one would believe me. I threw a book at him and chased him out the door. And as he walked to the car I screamed, 'I hope you die.'"

Nattie tried to speak, but with the first utterance Randi withdrew her hands and cradled her head in her folded arms on the table. Nattie gently stroked her forearm with her fingertips.

Randi finally raised her head. Her face was pale and her eyes red; she looked exhausted. "I'm sorry. I never do that."

"Well it was time, then."

Randi attempted to smile.

"You know, accidents don't happen because a twelve-year-old yells at her brother."

Randi made no response.

"I know that you said what you said, but it was a coincidence. You did not cause that accident."

Randi nodded, but Nattie could not tell if she believed her. "Have you told this to your therapist?"

"No, I just remembered it."

Nattie took her hand again and softly said, "I think maybe you should." This could be another cause of your sleep problems.

"I'm sorry to bother you guys," the waitress said tentatively. "It's almost midnight and I'm going home."

46

"Do you need us to leave?" asked Nattie, as Randi looked away and dabbed at her eyes with a tissue from her purse.

"No, you can stay, but I'd appreciate it if you could settle the check."

"Of course."

As Nattie opened her bag Randi handed the waitress a credit card. "Put it all on that."

Nattie protested. "You don't have to do that."

"I know. And you didn't have to listen to me all night."

"I was delighted." *On behalf of all the flat-chested twelve-year-old girls who froze out the girls with boobs, I owed it to you.*

Randi hugged Nattie in the parking lot. It was still awkward and stiff, but the firmness meant it was sincere. "You know, you would have been a great therapist."

"Thanks." It was too dark for the blushing to be visible.

"And as for Nathan and me, we were just available to each other at a time we both needed someone."

"So you and Nathan were just helping each other get through the night?"

"That's as good a way to put it as any."

"And now?"

"And now I don't need him like I did."

"So you aren't interested in him?"

"I didn't say that."

"Are you interested in him?"

"I would be if—"

"If what?"

"If he weren't in love with another woman."

CHAPTER 9

ELI ANDERSON
(very late Saturday night)

Nattie had no idea how long she had been asleep or even if she had been asleep at all, but something alerted her and she bolted upright. It was a noise, like the creaking furnace that had so frightened her the first time her parents left her alone to babysit her brother, Kevin. She sat very still, listening and watching, but hearing only the sound of her own breathing.

A shadow emerged from the kitchen and stood silhouetted against the dining room window. A stranger standing inside her dining room in the middle of the night was too frightening for her to feel scared. Instead time simply slowed down as she carefully leaned forward and reached for the revolver still holstered in the small of her back.

Then, as the shadow moved forward she quickly leveled the gun at the center of its chest. Instead of coming directly at Nattie the shadow crossed the living room and lay down on her couch.

She turned on the table lamp. "Do not move a single muscle, not a single hair!"

"Oh crap!" screamed a high, squeaky voice. The figure disobeyed her warning and leapt for the door.

48

"You stop right there," she shouted, "or I swear I will shoot you."

This time the shadow obeyed. Putting his hands over his head, he turned slowly to face her. The shadow was a young boy wearing baggy pants and a baggy Oakland Raiders sweatshirt. Clenching his jaw, he gave his best effort to hide his fear, but his eyes were glassy. "I did not hurt anything."

Standing up and keeping the gun pointed at his chest, Nattie motioned toward the sofa. "Fold your hands in front of you and sit down."

"Please don't shoot me." His voice cracked. "I'm only thirteen."

"Sit down! Now!"

He sighed, sat down on the edge of the sofa, and folded his arms.

She stepped a little closer to him and raised the gun barrel at his face. "We are going to get along much better if you do exactly as I say."

He looked confused as he stared at the gun.

"Fold…your…hands…on your lap."

Flinching, he complied.

"Good," she said in a more relaxed tone. She sat down on an ottoman across the coffee table from him. "Now, we are going to have a conversation. Is that clear?"

He nodded.

"What is your name?"

"Are you going to call the police?"

"Probably. Now tell me your name."

He stared at her. A hardened intruder would have refused to cooperate with her as long as she was going to call the police anyway. "Eli. Eli Anderson."

"OK. That's better. Now Eli, tell me, do you have a weapon?"

He vigorously shook his head. "I don't even have a knife."

Leaning forward, she narrowed her eyes, "Do I have to search you?"

"You can search me; really, I don't have anything."

Nattie knew that Hiram, her old boss and mentor, would have told her she was crazy; but she decided to trust what Eli told her. "OK, Eli, I believe you, and I am going to put down this gun."

"Thank you."

"But you just sit there and keep your hands folded. Do you understand?"

He nodded.

"How did you get in here, Eli?"

"Your kitchen door is broken."

"I know. That's why I keep it locked all the time. I never go in or out that way."

He hesitated, as if he were considering what to say. "It locks on the inside, but not the outside."

"That's good to know, but how did you come to discover this piece of information?"

"Can I go to the bathroom?"

"No."

"But I can't wait."

"Then you should have broken into someone else's home."

He slouched. "I was at Blackbird Bakery and I heard this guy talking on the phone. He said you were going to be on a case in Washington for a few days, so I knew you would not be home."

"What guy?"

"I don't know who he was."

"But he referred to me and you knew where I lived?"

"I knew who you were because of that story in the newspaper."

"You mean the one when I got into the fight in the bar?"

He shook his head. "No, when someone knocked you out in a parking lot."

She sighed.

"How many private investigators named Natasha could there be in Bristol?"

"So you figured out who I was from the paper and decided to break into my house because it was going to be empty."

"I got the address from the phone book." Sitting up again, he added, "I wasn't planning to break in when I heard him talking. I just needed a place to stay in a hurry and remembered your house was empty."

"So you broke in."

"But I didn't hurt anything," he pleaded. "I slept on the couch and left before it got light out."

"Why would you need a place to stay in a hurry?"

He looked down. "I don't want to talk about that."

50

"Oh," she said sweetly. "I don't want you to do anything you don't want to do. Would you like me to make you some pancakes?"

The smile on his face disappeared quickly when he raised his head and realized she was being sarcastic.

"You can tell me or you can tell the police, Eli. You pick."

He slouched back again. "It's my mother. My butthole of a father left her a year ago, but she lets him come home whenever he wants to be with her."

"And you can't stay home when he's there?"

"I could, but when he's done with her he's gonna want to leave and she's gonna to try to get him to stay."

Nattie watched him struggle with what to say next.

"That's when it gets ugly."

"Does he hurt her, Eli?"

The boy turned his head, but not before Nattie saw his eyes pool up with tears.

She let him catch his breath before asking, "How often does this happen, Eli?"

"Couple of times a month."

"That's a lot. Where do you stay when I'm not out of town?"

He glanced at her out of the corner of his eye, but did not answer.

Then, as if a light suddenly went on, she cried out, "Oh my stars, Eli. Have you ever stayed here when I was home?"

He shrugged.

"You have, haven't you? You have slept on my sofa when I was upstairs." *There's an ace detective for you. I've had an intruder stay with me repeatedly, and I haven't noticed a thing.*

Eli stared at her silently.

What the hell, she thought. "Eli, I'm going to bed. You can finish the night out on the sofa but—and I want you to listen to me very carefully. This is the last time."

He grinned.

"I'm serious, Eli. This is it, the last time. I'm calling my office manager first thing in the morning and getting that door fixed."

"Thank you, ma'am." He stood and held his hand out.

51

She stood and made a show of holstering her gun before shaking his hand. "I'm only thirty, Eli. If you call me 'ma'am' again, I'm going to shoot you. OK?"

"Yes, maaaa…."

She awoke to the smell of coffee the next morning. Descending the stairs in her robe, she heard Eli call out, "How do you drink your coffee?"

"Just Splenda."

"Black and sweet, coming right up."

She sat down at the kitchen table and watched as Eli scooped what had to be pancake batter from a bowl onto the griddle.

"What are you doing?"

"Pancakes," he answered as he set a mug of coffee on the table in front of her. "I hope you like it strong. My momma likes it strong."

"Strong is fine, and thank you. But why are you still here?"

"I'm making breakfast."

"I can see that, but I thought I made myself perfectly clear—"

"I know," he interrupted. "This is the last time. But since you couldn't make pancakes last night, I thought I'd help you out. You know, kind of a thank you for not calling the police."

You should thank me for not shooting you.

"I thought about making breakfast and bringing it to you in bed, but I was afraid you might not like being waked up."

"Woken up."

He nodded and slid a spatula under the corner of one of the pancakes.

"I didn't want to wake you and make you mad."

While she took a sip of coffee, she winked at him and pointed her finger at him as if it were a gun.

"I didn't want to get shot either," he added.

"This coffee tastes good. I didn't have any fancy coffees here. Where did it come from?"

He answered while flipping the pancakes. "It's the coffee you had in the refrigerator. I just added a pinch of cinnamon to the grounds."

"It's very good."

He smiled, "Are you going to want another stack?"

52

I don't really want this one, she thought. Pancakes for breakfast was reserved for the weekend. "No thanks, one stack is plenty."

"In that case do you mind if I—" He finished his question by gesturing at the griddle with his thumb.

"By all means, join me."

Nattie was half-finished with her stack when Eli sat down across from her with his.

"Where did you learn how to cook?"

"At home. My momma was a chef before she started writing."

"Well you make great pancakes."

"And coffee?"

"Yes, coffee too."

Eli took a big bite and smiled at Nattie as he chewed. Just before he swallowed, he asked, "Aren't you going to ask who my momma is?"

"Sure, I'll ask. Who is your mother?"

"Annabelle Ashley Anderson."

"The writer," Nattie replied feebly. She had no idea who Annabelle Ashley Anderson was, but clearly read Eli's expectation that she would.

"She writes cookbooks."

Nattie smiled and nodded.

After taking another huge bite of pancakes, Eli stood and retrieved two books from Nattie's bookshelf. He placed them on the table and sat back down.

"Oh my goodness. Your mother is Delia Davenport. I absolutely love her." Nattie held up *Dinner With Delia* and for the first time noticed the author's name, Annabelle Ashley Anderson. "I'm no cook, but what I know I learned from her. She is a great teacher. She makes things so simple. I can't believe it. Delia Davenport lives in Bristol. And she is your mother."

"Annabelle Ashley," he corrected her.

"Annabelle Ashley Anderson," she repeated. As her own celebrity awe waned she noticed the considerable pride Eli had in his mother and then wondered, *How does a woman as together as Delia Davenport do this to her son? How does a woman as together as Delia Davenport let a man treat her that way?* Then, with almost perfect timing, she happened to look at a wedding picture on her bookshelf. In the picture she stood with her alcoholic father on her right and her alcoholic ex-husband on her left. *Who do you think you're kidding?* she asked herself.

With significantly less enthusiasm than just a moment earlier, she picked up her copy of *Dinner With Delia*. "I learned how to cook from your mother. This was the only cookbook I have ever seen that does not use jargon." Laughing, she confessed, "I don't know what folding in an egg means."

"Oh, you separate the yolk from the white, then beat the white until it gets kind of foamy," With his hand he mimed the action: a slice followed by a scoop followed by a fold. "Then you mix it in like this so you don't lose all the air you beat in."

"Are you sure you're thirteen?"

A bashful smiled crossed his face. He pointed at the cookbook. "Can I see that for a moment?"

Nattie slid the book across to him. "Of course."

He thumbed through the book. "This isn't really my recipe, but it was my idea to add M&M'S to the pancakes and she gave me credit." He found the page he was looking for and held it open for Nattie to see.

Nattie read the words out loud, "'Replacing chocolate chips with M&M'S was a contribution of Eli, my eight-year-old son.' That's very impressive."

He beamed and retracted the book. As he did so, something small fell from the pages and landed in his lap. "What is this? He held out a small silver colored metal disc.

She had no idea what he was holding until she leaned closer. What she saw caught her off guard for a moment, but she quickly got her breath. She removed it from his palm. "That's a slug."

"A slug?"

She took a long measured look at it. "When an electrician puts a new electrical junction box in, he has to punch out some discs so that the wires can get in. This is one of those discs. When I was a kid we used to pretend it was money."

He frowned, "Why was it in the book?"

"It was a joke my ex-husband used to play on me," she lied. "He would put it in whatever book I was reading and it would fall in my lap."

"That's nice."

"What's nice?"

"It's nice that he tried to be funny."

It would have been nice if he tried other things as well. "That was nice," she agreed out loud.

CHAPTER 10

KEVIN GIVES PRAYER ADVICE
(Sunday lunch)

"I'd say, just go ahead and steal it." The remark was not uttered with malice or even defiance. It was spoken with the same emotional intensity that one might say, "It looks like it's going to rain," or, "David Letterman was funny last night." In fact, when he said it, Kevin never looked up from his place at the table where he was spooning some Ribollita onto the end of a slice of ciabatta bread.

His obliviousness to the ensuing silence was broken when he leaned forward to take a bite from the dripping end of his bread and discovered all eyes focused on him.

"I like it this way," he explained, apparently assuming that his table manners were the issue at hand.

Nattie could not tell if he was unaware of what he had said or if he was unaware that he had said it out loud.

At the end of the table to Nattie's right sat Lionel, their stepfather. Rather than glaring with disapproval as Nattie would have expected, he sat there dumbfounded. Not that others weren't glaring. At the other end of the lunch table both Ingrid, their mother, and Samantha, their stepsister, both had their glares on. Samantha sat across from Kevin with her son, Trevor, to her left Her husband, Eric Gorzilanski, sat on the other side of Trevor. Eric, the only person at the dining room table who was not focused on Kevin, was scowling at his son, who was giggling in amusement at Kevin's advice. The scowl, however, struck Nattie as insincere, as if Eric were struggling not to smile himself.

No one at the table, including Kevin, who had given the advice, thought for a moment that Trevor might just do what Kevin suggested and steal the iPad 2. Correcting Kevin's influence on Trevor was not, therefore, the concern. Correcting Kevin himself was the concern.

"Stop that," snapped Samantha when she finally noticed how much her son was enjoying the irreverence.

Trevor stopped laughing immediately and, after a quick glance at his mother, turned toward his father. Nattie wondered if the subtle unspoken message between father and son might have been, "We'll laugh about this later."

The curt, "What were you thinking, Kevin?" from Ingrid drew Nattie's attention back to Kevin.

"What do you mean?"

Kevin's question sounded ridiculous to Nattie until his glance around the table finally reached her, and she realized that he really did not know what was wrong with what he had said.

"You told Trev to steal an iPad." It was Samantha's turn to scowl. "Do you really need someone to tell you what was wrong with that?"

Looking at his nephew, Kevin pleaded, "Trevor, did you think I meant that you should really steal anything?"

"No," answered Trevor immediately. After catching his mother's reaction out of the corner of his eye he looked back to his father.

"That is not exactly the point, Kevin," explained Lionel in his calm, "I am about to swing into lecture mode" voice.

"Well, what is the point?" asked Kevin, directing his question at Ingrid in an attempt to control where the lecture came from.

While Ingrid rolled her eyes, Samantha exhaled deeply, communicating that her displeasure with Kevin had not yet diminished and was not likely to diminish anytime soon.

"I know what I said would have sounded awful out of context, but come on, everybody, give me a break." Pointing across the table, he added, "Trevor knows not to take that out of context, don't you, Trev?"

This time Trevor did not answer beyond shrugging his shoulders.

"OK, Kevin," interjected Lionel, the lawyer. "Why don't you walk us through the conversation so you can remind us of the context?"

Don't do it, thought Nattie, *it's a lawyer trick*. He's going to get you to hang yourself with your own testimony.

"OK," agreed Kevin and began his verbal journey into the bear trap. "Trevor asked for a new iPad, right?"

Lionel nodded his agreement then placed his elbows on the table and folded his hands across his face. To Nattie he looked like he was readying himself for the kill, for that moment when Kevin's account of the conversation fully exposed his guilt.

"And when he got no answer, Trevor tried to justify his desire for the iPad with something that had to do with school. By the way, Trev, I thought that was a good strategy."

Trevor knit his eyebrows as if to say to his parents, *I don't know what he's talking about*, but to Kevin, *Why are you revealing my best technique?*

"Anyway," Kevin continued, ignoring Trevor's response, "he was then told that he already had a computer and if he wanted another one he would have to use his own money."

Lionel nodded his agreement with Kevin's recollection again.

"Then Trevor complained that he had no job and no way to make money." Kevin pointed at Samantha. "That's when Sammie told him he should pray about it."

Upon hearing herself referred to as "Sammie," Samantha stiffened her back enough to raise her height several inches. When they were younger, Samantha preferred her full name or occasionally just Sam, but Sammie was never acceptable until her senior year of high school when she began dating Teddy Baker. Teddy called her "Mammie Sammie from Miami," and the name was suddenly OK. But when Lionel had made fun of the title, that was it for Samantha. She ended the relationship with Teddy Baker and the name "Sammie" became off limits once again.

The name brought back happy memories for Kevin and Nattie. It was during this half year that Samantha was the friendliest to them. They both really liked Teddy and they liked the way he treated them as her siblings. Mostly they liked the way he treated her, for even though she was often a stick in the mud and behaved as if they were beneath her, she was still family and they wished the best for her. "Mammie Sammie from Miami" was still how they referred to her when they were alone, and the reference was affectionately playful.

"That's when you told him to just steal it," bristled Samantha.

"You told him to pray about it first," responded Kevin.

"I fail to see where you are taking us with this," came Lionel's solemn voice from the end of the table. His hands were folded on the edge of the table. He no longer looked like a lion waiting to pounce on his prey. Now he had the look of a lion whose prey was snatched up and carried off by an eagle.

"Well," explained Kevin, "she invoked a religious practice that, as I understand it, is a well-recognized Christian strategy. Am I wrong?"

Lionel bristled. "I'm not sure the word 'strategy' is the right word."

"But it is something that Christians often say to each other about problems they face. Isn't it?"

Nattie could not help but recognize that the lawyer was being cross-examined.

"Of course," answered Samantha, "Prayer is something Christians believe in and encourage in one another."

"But do you really believe that God is going to give Trevor an iPad if he prays for it?"

Samantha nearly exploded. "I'm not going to listen to you degrade prayer."

Kevin held his hands up in a defensive position. "I'm not degrading prayer. It is a powerful tool in the hands of mortals."

"Yes, it is," agreed Lionel. "Please continue."

Nattie smiled. The lawyer is back.

"But prayer is too powerful for us to handle. How could God just allow us to get whatever we ask for? Can you imagine what the world would be like if we all got whatever we prayed for?"

Samantha's fidgeting betrayed her frustration with Kevin's argument and her inability to defeat it. She looked at Lionel, desperately hoping he would put Kevin in his place.

"You make a good point," conceded Lionel, "but I still fail to see where you are going."

Kevin grinned. "Well, since we all agree that Trevor cannot count on getting his iPad by praying for it, he can count on another tried and true Christian practice while actually getting the iPad."

"By stealing it," Samantha said sarcastically.

"Yes," Kevin replied, sitting back and spreading his hands. "And when he gets caught, he can ask for forgiveness."

CHAPTER 11

BREAKFAST WITH DEB

"I've never driven to Abingdon this way before," noted Debbie from the passenger seat of Nattie's Subaru Forester. "It's pretty."

"It is," agreed Nattie.

The back way from Bristol to Abingdon always took a bit longer than getting on Route 81; but it could take much, much longer if there was a farm vehicle ahead of you, especially if it was hauling spools of hay. They were lucky today and had Old Jonesboro Road to themselves.

Pointing to the fenced-in plot on her right, Nattie said, "There used to be a long-horned steer that they kept in there, but I haven't seen it in a while. It would always lie down near that fence."

When Nattie and Nathan were dating, Abingdon was a favorite place to go for the evening. For dinner Nathan preferred the Tavern or the Martha Washington Inn, while Nattie's favorite spot was the Wildflower Bakery. When Nathan proposed to her, it was at the Wildflower Bakery just before they were supposed to go to the Barter Theater to see the Christmas show.

Nathan especially liked taking the back way to Abingdon because at the intersection where they turned to get to Exit 13 of Route 81 there was a plot of land with a log cabin on it. Nathan always referred to it as "our cabin." It was a dream that was still alive in her to some extent; otherwise, she would never take the long way to Abingdon. But the warm dream was bittersweet. If she and Nathan were still together and if they bought "their cabin," she, not he, would do all the extra chores that owning such a place would mean. Still, seeing it on her left as she made the turn that would take them under route 81 and on to Lee Highway brought familiar warmth to her chest.

Passing Alison's Restaurant on her right, Nattie remarked, "They have the best loaded baked potato soup there."

"Do you have a favorite thing to order everywhere?"

Nattie shrugged. "Is that bad?"

"No, it's just interesting. Most women I know aren't honest about their fixation with food."

"Wow. Fixation! That's a strong word."

"Oh, did I use the wrong word? I thought of saying obsession but I thought fixation sounded better. I thought fascination was too strong."

"Actually, I think it might be the other way, with obsession being stronger than fascination and fixation being stronger than obsession."

"I am sorry, then. I meant fascination."

"No apology is necessary. Besides, fixation is probably more accurate. And to set the record straight, I don't just have one favorite thing at Alison's. I'll be meeting a couple of detectives from Washington County there this evening, and besides the soup, I'm looking forward to the hot bread and herb butter they bring to the table at night."

"Thyme?"

"It's after ten."

"No, I mean is thyme the herb in the butter?"

The downtown area of Abingdon looked like a Norman Rockwell painting. Many of the businesses that lined either side of the street, especially east of the Martha Washington Inn and the Barter Theater across the street, were in old homes that looked like they could have housed Mark Twain at one time. Zazzy'z Café and Bookstore was in one of the last such homes on the eastern end of the downtown area.

It was 10:30 when they got to Zazzy'z so the breakfast and go-to-work crowd was long gone and the lunch crowd was not yet hungry. Besides the two elderly gentlemen holding court on the deck outside, Nattie and Debbie were the only customers in the quaint café behind the bookstore. The room was split with four short tables on one side of the aisle between the door and the counter. Three tall tables and chairs were on the other side of the aisle.

Both women scrutinized the array of sandwiches, wraps, and pastries through the small glass case to the right of the counter before ordering "just coffee."

"Would you like to split something?" asked the young woman behind the counter who had been watching them. Her nametag said Sammi, not to be confused with Mammie Sammie from Miami.

"I want to split everything," confessed Debbie with a laugh, "that's the problem."

"Just coffee for now," added Nattie, "but thank you for offering."

Sammi smiled. "Bold?"

Turning toward Nattie and nodding at Sammi, Debbie observed, "She's got us pegged."

"I think she means the coffee."

Debbie looked back at Sammi who motioned her agreement. "I was just teasing, honey. I'll have the bold."

"Can I have a bold coffee but switch to decaf if I get a refill?"

"Sure. The first refill is free as long as you're not using a to-go cup."

While Sammi got their coffee, Debbie leaned closer to Nattie and whispered through a crooked grin, "You want to switch to decaf before you even taste the bold. You're kinda pushy, aren't you?"

"I'd say you're the pushy one. I think of myself as—"

"Bold," they said together. They were still grinning when Sammi returned with their coffee cups.

"I got this," said Debbie and handed Sammi a five-dollar bill.

"That's $4. 93. Do you have three cents?"

"I do," responded Nattie quickly and reached into her pocket.

Holding out the contents of her pocket Nattie let Debbie dig out the three pennies from her palm.

"What's that?" asked Debbie while she pointed at Nathan's slug Nattie had forgotten was still in her pocket.

Noticing Nattie's hesitation the deer-in-the-headlights expression on her face, Debbie softly withdrew her question. "It's OK, forget I asked."

Without speaking Nattie pointed at a table on the short table side of the room and went to sit down.

Being asked a question about an intimate part of her life was unfamiliar territory for Nattie. She was almost always the questioner, the listener. Maybe it was the sudden reminder of the memory in the kitchen with Eli. Maybe it was her growing trust in Debbie. Maybe it was simply time to tell the story to someone. Her decision to open up the tender memory may have even had something to do with where they were at that precise moment.

"It's a slug from an electrical junction box," explained Nattie after they were both settled at their table in the corner. The slug was still in her palm. Looking at it, she continued, "It's something my ex-husband gave me a long time ago. I'd forgotten about it until it fell out of a cookbook the other day. I was busy with something when I found it, so I just stuck it in my pocket. I guess I forgot about it again."

"It looks like it's pretty important to you."

"It was," confessed Nattie. Then looking at it again, she added, "It is."

Debbie took a long sip from the edge of her cup.

With the slug put safely back in her pocket Nattie took a long sip from her cup too and began her story, "Nathan is a dreamer." Which is adorable on little boys. "That was his slug. He told me the story of how he got it a few days after he asked me to marry him." Nattie's face lit up with recognition. She pointed at one of the tall tables across the aisle. "As a matter of fact, I think we were sitting right over there when he told me the story. We happened to be in the bookstore when there was an author here signing her cookbooks. Nate bought me one and had her sign it, 'To the slug of Nathan's life.'

Debbie's face contorted involuntarily. She laughed, however, when Nattie added, "I'm pretty sure I looked like you just did when I read it, but then he told me the story of the slug."

"I have no idea how this is going to turn out, but I'm all ears."

"It seems my Nathan was a bit on the gullible side as a boy." Not that it ever changed. "One day he met a couple of older boys who took a liking to his brand new baseball glove, so they concocted a story about this magic slug they had."

"Oh, you are kidding me. He pulled a Jack and the Beanstalk and traded the family cow for some magic beans."

"I hadn't thought of it that way, but you're right, that's exactly what he did. No beans, but that glove was genuine cowhide."

Deb gestured at Nattie with her coffee cup. "And you were the bean stalk?"

Glancing over toward the tall chairs brought the memory more into focus. "He told me he felt so foolish that had never told anyone about it. He told his folks he lost the glove. And he always kept the slug to remind him never to believe in magic again." Nattie took another long sip from her coffee. The words that followed were spoken more slowly and more deeply. Debbie showed no sign of noticing the change. "He told himself that he was going to hang on to that slug until the day came when he believed in magic again."

Debbie put her cup down. "And that day came."

"When I said yes."

CHAPTER 12

DINNER WITH HENRY AT ALISON'S

Alison's Restaurant, located on the south side of Lee Highway at the far western edge of Abingdon, was once a drive-in. Originally, diners drove under an overhang extending from an outside eating area at the back of the building, away from the street. The interior, which did not appear to have been designed for inside dining, was now packed with tables, a few placed here and a few there, every nook and cranny used for something. As a building it was unimpressive. The outside needed a coat of paint, but then again it needed a coat of paint ten years earlier too. In spite of all the architectural flaws it was always crowded.

Henry was already there when Nattie entered. He sat in the dining area directly across from the front door. His wave as soon as she was inside the door was so enthusiastic that it felt as if he were hurrying her rather than merely trying to catch her attention.

"Miss McMorales," he announced with a tip of his head as she approached the table. Instead of standing, which she didn't really expect, he raised himself a few inches off his seat, a move he could not maintain and one that did nothing more than draw attention to the fact that he was not standing. He had probably tried to extend his hand as a gesture offering her the seat across from where he sat, but as he fell back into his seat, the gesture looked more like a command that she sit there immediately.

"Shall I sit here?" she asked with as much innocence in her voice as she could muster.

"Please," he said more graciously from a fully seated position. "Have you ever eaten here before?"

"Several times."

"Well, one of the things they do here is bring a hot loaf of bread to the table."

"I have had it many times."

"And the herb butter they bring with the bread is their own secret recipe." He extended the small wooden cutting board with what was left of the five-inch loaf on top. "You have to try a piece."

Nattie placed the bread board on the table next to her and took a second look at it. Rather than slicing the bread from the end of the loaf, Henry had cut horizontally and taken the upper two thirds, leaving just a stump for the rest of the table.

"I just love this bread. Go ahead, try it. And try that herb butter; it really makes it."

Turning her attention to the little plastic cup of herb butter Nattie estimated about ten percent remained.

"I need a lot of that for the top crusty part," he explained.

"I understand."

"Miss McMorales?"

The voice startled her. It came from a man standing beside her. Her attention was so focused on Henry that she had not noticed him approaching. The speaker, whom Nattie guessed to be in his sixties, was a smallish man with the thinning gray hair and the suit and tie and mismatched vest. She doubted if his sense of style had ever been in fashion or effective.

"Detective Schneider?"

He bowed his head. "Douglas Schneider at your service."

Nattie wondered if at some other time in his life he clicked his heels together when he made his head bob like that.

"Duke Schneider." Henry's laugh sound more like a snort.

"Duke," said Nattie as she extended her hand, "I'm Nattie Moreland."

Henry openly laughed as Detective Schneider took her hand.

"Don't mind him," the detective muttered. "He's referring to Duke Snyder."

Nattie could tell that both the men expected her to recognize the name, but she had no idea, which meant it was either a sports name or a name everyone thirty years older than she would know. "I'm sorry, is that a football player?"

Both men laughed.

"Baseball," Henry informed her, "Duke Snyder played second base for the old Brooklyn Dodgers. He was unquestionably the greatest second baseman ever to play the game."

"I'll bet he could really hit that ball," she said in her best "you must think I know nothing about baseball because I'm a woman" voice.

As Douglas Schneider took the seat next to her, she added, "How does he compare to Ryne Sandberg?" This she asked in her own voice.

Detective Schneider eyed her, noting she was not the baseball illiterate she had sounded like a moment before.

"Ryne Sandberg was a good ballplayer, but most women liked him more because he was a pretty boy than because of his skill."

"And yet Ryno was the second baseman for the National League's All-Star team eight consecutive years. How does that compare to your Mr. Snyder?" It was a bluff. Nattie had no idea how many years Ryno had made the All-Star team. She knew that neither man would call her on it unless they were sure beyond a shadow of a doubt lest they risk losing this pissing contest.

"I think Nattie here is a Cub fan, Henry."

"My condolences."

"Thank you," she said politely. "My grandfather always said, 'It takes more faith to be a Cub fan.'"

"A wise man, your Grandfather."

"Thank you, Detective Schneider."

"Please," he smiled warmly, "I'd be honored if you would call me Duke."

Nattie was confused. "I thought he was joking when he called you Duke."

"He was," Duke said with a twinkle in his eye that made his sense of fashion suddenly seem perfect.

A waitress brought three water glasses and menus to the table. She also passed out little slips of paper listing the daily specials. Nattie had no need to open the menu. She would be ordering the baked potato soup and a side salad. She knew this would be her order when Henry had called her and suggested they meet with detective Schneider, who, he claimed, would have information about a suspect that would "open your eyes." While the two men read their menus, Nattie killed time by glancing over the daily specials. the Balsamic Burger caught her eye. It had blue cheese crumbles, sun dried tomatoes, and was served on grilled rye bread. The description reminded her of a steak prepared in a balsamic reduction she once had in Tuscany while she was tracking down Ollie Ruggiliano's runaway fiancée, Adelle Quinlin. It was the best steak she had ever had. She ordered the burger.

Dinner was a mixture of good food and tedious conversation. Although the burger was tasty, the balsamic flavor was added after cooking, not the Italian way. Duke, to his credit, made several attempts to engage Nattie but all but one ended up as fodder for Henry to demonstrate his authoritative opinions. The singular topic Nattie was allowed to answer for herself was of course the inquiry into the name Natasha McMorales. *I have got to come up with a better story,* Nattie told herself for the umpteenth time.

"Gentlemen," Nattie began, "this has been interesting, but if you don't mind, I'd like to get down to business."

Duke cleared his throat, as if to begin, but Henry cut him off. "Since we are both investigating the attack on Frank Lester, I thought it would be good to begin on the right foot. There is no reason that we cannot cooperate with each other."

Nattie agreed. "I don't usually get such eager cooperation. I usually get the information I need from the police investigation but I always have to ask for it first, so I appreciate your taking the initiative very much." *But I wonder why.*

"First off, I think there are things you need to know about our victim."

"Mr. Lester?" she asked, knowing the answer, as she looked first at Henry then at Duke, who remained silent and redirected her back to Henry with his eyes.

"Frank Lester is not a Boy Scout. We have a file full of complaints about him."

"What kind of complaints?"

"Basically, he is a bully. He has never gone so far that we could get a real solid conviction on him, but he has left a long list of people who are fearful of him. In the past ten years there have been four restraining orders filed by different people against him. All were dropped after the first sixty days."

"It takes a hearing to extend it after sixty days," explained Duke.

"But four filings by four different people in ten years is hard to ignore."

Duke answered this one. "We'll get that many and more from one person, usually the wife or a neighbor, but four different people is really unusual."

"Was one of them his wife?"

"Nope," answered Henry, "but that doesn't mean he's not terrorizing her. If she's being abused, and I'll bet you anything she is, it might take a while for her to report it. It may not make sense, but that's just how it works."

"So you think Randi Lester is being abused?"

"I can't prove it, but yep, she's being abused."

Nattie took a long look at each man while each of them watched her closely for her reaction. "Is Randi Lester the suspect you had information about?"

"Mrs. Lester is not a suspect as far as I'm concerned," Henry replied.

Nattie turned to Duke for his opinion. "And you?"

Duke waved both hands, "It's not my case."

"This has all the earmarks of a vigilante cop," Henry stated emphatically and then held his silence.

Nattie instinctively slowed everything down. She had not expected what she heard, but the gravity of it was not lost on her. She knew Henry was waiting for her; but she also knew he could not remain silent, even when he had nothing to say. His silence now must have taken all the self-restraint he had within him.

The self-restraint didn't last long. "Clearly," Henry began again, "someone was taking justice into their own hands. We don't know who. And we don't know what for. But Lester was not robbed or violated." He tapped his finger on the table. "He was punished."

"OK," Nattie conceded, "he was punished. But the list of people who would like to see him punished is probably pretty large. I only met him once, and he was in a hospital bed, but I'd like to see him punished." It was her turn to wait for a response but neither man found her confession noteworthy. "Why do you think it was a cop?"

"Control," answered Henry immediately. "Do you know what kind of force it takes to break a thigh bone?" Without waiting for an answer, he added, "Plenty, but if the vigilante was angry, out of control, Frank Lester would be dead. Whoever did this was strong enough to strangle him into unconsciousness. You can take it to the bank, Frank Lester struggled."

"And this guy had the wherewithal to have knocked his head off."

"But he didn't," continued Henry. "He hit him exactly hard enough to break bones, but had enough control that he didn't hit him where it would have killed him." Henry sat back, laying his hands flat on the table. "When Frankie Boy was safely unconscious, this guy turned loose the dogs, but didn't kill him. Now I ask you, who has that kind of control over their use of force?" Henry leaned forward and tapped his index finger on the table. "Cops. That's who."

"Do you just think it was some random cop, or do you have someone specific in mind?"

Henry just smiled. Apparently, he was still too enamored with his performance to answer.

"Do you?" she asked Duke.

Duke turned toward Henry. Both men had grown more serious by several degrees. After Henry nodded his permission, Duke reached inside his jacket, withdrew a photograph, and laid it before her. "Do you know this man?"

The man he referred to looked fifteen years younger, fifty pounds lighter, and completely out of character, with short hair and a police uniform. But there was no mistaking who it was. Their prime suspect was Beau Robinette.

CHAPTER 13

NATTIE PULLS AN ALL-NIGHTER

I hate this, thought Nattie as she sat in the foyer of the Gray home. Facing the foyer was a large open living room with an ample supply of comfortable seating; but she was not there socially so the bench in the foyer would have to do. To the right of the living room were double sliding doors leading to the library. The doors were shut. Behind the doors Mr. and Mrs. Gray were in conference.

"Wait here," Mrs. Gray had instructed her before marching into the library, armed with the packet of photos Nattie had handed her, to confront her husband about his infidelity.

Mr. Gray had routinely "traveled" on business only to return early the next morning with no luggage, so Mrs. Gray hired Nattie to discover what the word "travel" meant. Two all-nighters was all it took for Nattie to have photographic proof that "traveling" meant spending the night with a woman from his office.

Mrs. Gray had asked Nattie to wait, promising to pay her when she returned. Nattie was used to waiting to receive payment for her services and would have been fine if Mrs. Gray had sent the check at her convenience. She would even have preferred that. This waiting was different. Nattie knew that the real reason Mrs. Gray had asked her to wait was to provide additional evidence against Mr. Gray, as if the photographs were not enough.

So Nattie waited and did what she often did when she waited, constructing a top ten list. The list she worked on in her head over the last two all-nighters was of favorite smells. As she sat there she began to type the list into her iPhone "notes" application:

Babies after bath time
Puppy breath
Cut grass
A steak cooking on a grill in the distance
The earth after a night of heavy rain
Honeysuckle
A wood fire on a drizzly day
Bacon and onions on a grill
Cinnamon buns baking

She was trying to remember the after-shave her grandfather, the Wolf, wore when the doors opened and out stormed Mr. Gray. The fact that it was he and not his wife that emerged was evidence enough that the conversation had not gone well. If Mr. Gray had confessed, then they might have gotten to a place where they could start the slow process of rebuilding their marriage. Nattie had seen it before with another client, Mrs. Jane. Confronting Mr. Jane's affair forced them to face and fix problems in their marriage they had ignored for years. They were, in a manner of speaking, thankful.

Mr. Gray's being the first one from the library was not a good sign and neither was his demeanor. With a reddened face and his lower teeth bared, he barked at her, "How do you live with yourself?"

Having no answer that would have satisfied him Nattie sat quietly and waited. The wait was short. He spit on her, threw the front door open, and stomped out.

With his spit on her shoulder, Nattie watched him march across their front lawn. *Sometimes I hate my job.*

CHAPTER 14

KEVIN WORKS HIS MAGIC

"How did it go?"

"I suppose that depends on your point of view. You saw the pictures. I got what she paid me to get."

"And you got paid."

She put the check on Kevin's desk. "And I got spit on."

Kevin immediately stood up and squared his shoulders toward his sister. Had she given him the slightest signal that she was open to a hug, he was ready.

"I'm OK," she said, looking away. "He was just angry he got caught."

"I'm sorry, Sarge. He had no business doing that. He was guilty."

Nattie shrugged. "I know. He was plenty guilty. And she deserved to know. But being blamed, even when you know you're right, still hurts."

Kevin made a fist and threw a mock punch. "Why didn't you bloody his nose for him?"

Oddly, she had thought several times of punching Mr. Gray, but each time had been when she caught him cheating on his wife, a woman she hardly knew. "I didn't think of it," she answered.

Kevin sat back down in front of his computer. "Well, I found that therapist you wanted me to track down."

"Wow, that was fast." After her dinner with the Washington County "Mounties," Nattie had called the office and left a message for Kevin to research an Asoph Saylor, PhD, of New Orleans.

"He's not in practice anymore. He's a writer now. Have you ever heard of the book, *The Real McGoo*?"

She shook her head.

"He wrote it. I think it won some awards."

She said, "Order it," simultaneously as he said, "I ordered it."

Kevin grinned at their harmony and held up his palm for her to high-five, which she accommodated.

"According to the Internet he has a pretty predictable morning routine. He goes for a walk on the Riverwalk, which is along the Mississippi right by the French Quarter. And he always ends up at Café Du Monde around eight o'clock."

"Nice work, Kevin."

"I thought you might read his book on the plane and approach him like a reader. He's a writer so I assume he'd be open to hearing from a fan."

"Good plan. I just may use it. By the way, Kevin, do you know anything about an old-time second baseman named Duke Snyder?"

"Of course. Duke Snyder, the Silver Fox, the Duke of Flatbush. He's got one of those names you don't forget. But he wasn't a second baseman. He was a center fielder. Why?"

"Just curious," she said through a wry smile.

CHAPTER 15

PENTACOST SUNDAY

Nattie's flight from Tri-Cities to Atlanta and then to New Orleans was uneventful, as was the shuttle ride from the airport to her hotel, the Place D'Armes. Arriving at 11:00 a.m. for a 4:00 p.m. check-in was a snag but the concierge was accommodating and allowed her to change first into something more adapted to the ninety-five-degree humidity and then to store her luggage until she could get into her room.

Her first discovery of the day was of how centrally her hotel was located. If she turned right on Anne Street, she could walk a block and a half and be on Bourbon Street. To her left she could see Café Du Monde another block and a half away. Walking toward Café Du Monde she got as far as the first curb where she heard a jazz combo working the Sunday brunch at Muriel's Restaurant. There was almost no choice other than go inside.

It was Nattie's first real taste of New Orleans. The dining room looked as if it had once been the front room of a well to-do-resident of the French Quarter. She sat facing an interior courtyard teaming with greenery and sunlight. Just like the movies, she noted. She ordered a Midi Salad complete with champagne marinated tomatoes, avocado, and Feta cheese and for her main course Louisiana Alligator Hash.

After lunch she strolled around Jackson Square, marveling at the artists and palm readers spread out on the terrace in front of Saint Louis Basilica. *Now there's something you don't see very often in Bristol*, she thought as she watched a voodoo priest pose for pictures on the church steps.

Assuming she would find artwork, she followed people into the church where the air-conditioning was refreshing and the music was alluring. The cantor reminded her of Lorenna McKennitt. What she unwittingly had walked into was a special afternoon service held there every Pentecost Sunday. It was a confirmation service for 137 adult confirmands. She stayed for the short service, enjoying the cantor and the proud glances between the two young girls sitting in front of her and their father who sat with the other adult confirmands. After the service she discovered an oil painting of Saint Francis toward the front and, blending in with all the family photos being taken, managed to take a picture of the painting for her collection.

Returning to the Place D'Armes just after 4:00 p.m., Nattie found her room ready and her luggage waiting for her. On the way to her room she passed through three courtyards, each teaming with greenery and sunlight a la New Orleans. Then it was off for an early dinner at the Napoleon House, so named because the original owner offered it to Napoleon when he was exiled from France in 1821. Napoleon never made it but Earnest Hemingway did.

She returned to her room for a low-key evening to finish reading *The Real McGoo*. By lights out she had decided to wangle a meeting with Asoph Saylor using Kevin's plan, pretending to be not only a fan of Saylor's writing, but also the journalist Twila Pierce of the *Bristol Herald Courier*. As a reader she really had become a fan, and as a journalist she could easily ask for an extensive interview.

CHAPTER 16

NATTIE FINDS ASOPH SAYLOR AT CAFÉ DU MOND

The atmosphere of Jackson Square at seven o'clock in the morning differed greatly from that of the previous evening. The artists were missing from the Pedestrian Mall. In their place was a city worker spraying down the walkway and stone footing underneath the wrought-iron fence that bordered the park. The seventy-three degrees and gentle breeze felt cool compared to the sweltering ninety-five from the day before.

The portico of Café Du Monde was virtually empty when Nattie crossed Decatur Street. She was able to walk straight to the take-out window, order coffee and beignets, and have her pick of places to sit. In order to maintain the most advantageous view of the entire seating area, she picked a table in the corner farthest from the restaurant and closest to the street. With the park fence at her back and also on her left, no one inside the pavilion would be outside of her field of vision.

The first beignet in the bag was still warm. Biting it was a mixture of heavenly sweetness and messy frustration since a good portion of the powdered sugar ended up in her lap. She jerked forward so that the table might catch more of the sugar dropping from her mouth. The damage already having been done, the only effect of her movement was to put her in an awkward position when a slender black man began to serenade her from the other side to the fence.

He had parked his bicycle and set up his white plastic tip bucket while she was distracted. Now, with her body contorted over a pastry she did not know how to manage, he was singing to her. It had to be her he was singing to—she was the only person there. She turned toward him in hopes he would notice her hapless condition and stop drawing attention to them.

He only smiled more broadly and increased his volume. He then raised his hand and pointed toward the sky. This was a signal to her to avoid further eye contact.

Oh thank you, she said to herself when his singing attracted some other patrons for him to serenade.

It was a few minutes before 8:00 a.m. when Asoph Saylor entered the café from the backside of the pavilion. His barrel chest and muscular legs made him look even shorter than the five six his bio claimed him to be. Worn khaki shorts and a white shirt with a torn pocket contrasted sharply with his scuffless brand-new white cross-trainers. Removing his light brown cap, he glanced around looking for an open table.

Nattie studied him as he settled in. From where she sat, she could not tell if there was any gray in his short but ruffled sandy blond hair and scruffy beard, but she could tell that he reminded her of her father's father, James Johnson, the Cub fan she and Kevin affectionately referred to as the Wolf. Before sitting, Saylor whispered something to the waitress that made her smile. Then he slowly surveyed the people around his table, giving anyone who looked at him a smile and a nod.

His eyes twinkled. In Nattieland, this meant that he could be cerebrally playful without being sinister, sexual, or degrading. Nattie liked men whose eyes twinkled. She even knew two, both of them her grandfathers. There must be others; at least she hoped there were more than two. Duke Schneider might be one, but she did not know yet. Kevin's eyes twinkled, but he didn't count. In many ways he was still a little boy, and all boys had twinkling eyes. And Asoph Saylor, whom she

80

had not even met yet, could be one too. The thought gave her all she needed to draw her plan together.

After standing and brushing the powdered sugar off her lap, she threw a dollar bill in the white bucket. "God bless you," said the singer warmly.

"Mr. McGoo?" Nattie asked as she approached Asoph Saylor's table.

The writer put his pen down and closed the pocket Moleskine he was making notes in. A hearty chuckle shook his whole frame, and he greeted Nattie with eyes nearly closed shut by two plump cheeks that rose above his beard as if from a push-up bra. "I am, as a matter of fact, but no one is supposed to know that except my ex-wife."

Homerun.

"You've read *The Real McGoo*, I take it?"

"I have. Just finished it yesterday, in fact. I loved it."

He chuckled again. "Ah, you have said the magic words. And you did it graciously, without making me beg." He gestured at the open chair next to him. "Are you having café au lait and beignets?"

"Just coffee, I think, but I'd love to join you if you're sure you do not mind."

"How could I mind? Please, join me. I wrote *The Real McGoo* for you, after all."

"Me?"

"OK. Not just you. But you and the two hundred other people who have read it."

The waitress brought a mug of black coffee and sat it in front of him.

"Thank you, Wendy, and would you bring another for my new friend here?"

Wendy turned toward Nattie. "Do you want beignets?"

"Café au lait and beignets is what this establishment is known for," interjected Asoph. "It is one of the things every tourist who comes to the Big Easy must do, at least once."

"Maybe tomorrow, but for today I'll stay with the plain coffee and Splenda, please."

"The coffee is not plain," Wendy declared. "It's a French roast, made with chicory. Is that what you want?"

Nattie nodded. "Is that OK?"

Wendy put her hand on Nattie's shoulder. "This is the Big Easy, baby; you can have whatever you want."

When Wendy left, Asoph lifted a finger. "If you will excuse me for one moment, I need to finish jotting down a few notes."

He did not wait for Nattie's permission, but bent over his notebook and scribbled furiously for a while. He eyed something across the street for a moment. When he was satisfied with whatever he was looking for, he bobbed his head and went back to writing in his little book. Half a minute later he bobbed his head again and put the pen in his shirt pocket. Holding the closed Moleskine up for display, he waved it forward and backward, announcing, "These little notebooks are a writer's best friend."

"Moleskines," Nattie repeated, trying to impress him.

"Yes. They say Hemingway used them. That's probably how they can get away with charging what they charge for them."

"But that's not why you buy them." Nattie gently stroked his ego.

"True." He leaned over to slide the notebook into his back pocket. "I buy them because of how well they stand up to me sitting on them."

Asoph scooted his chair closer to the table. "Now that we are old friends, would you prefer for me to keep calling you my new friend, or is there some other name you would prefer?"

"I'm Natalie." In spite of her plan to call herself Twila Pierce, her real name came out of her mouth.

"Good to meet you Natalie." Asoph extended his hand. "I am, as you have already surmised, the real Mr. McGoo, but my driver's license says I am Asoph Saylor."

Nattie took his hand and gave him her maiden name, "Natalie Johnson."

"Good to meet you, Natalie Johnson. What brings you to New Orleans?"

"I'm afraid I don't have a very interesting reason for being here."

Wendy reappeared with Nattie's coffee, two packets of Splenda, and a small plate with what looked like three little brown pillows covered with a mound of powdered sugar.

"I guess you got the beignets anyway," he observed.

"How do I eat that without making a mess?"

"In a swimming pool." The eyes twinkled.

82

Forcing two of the pastries into her already sugar-overloaded system, Nattie held her cover while Asoph told her about New Orleans.

When she felt that she had eaten enough, Nattie pushed the remaining beignet to the other side of the table and began brushing the powered sugar from her shirt.

"So, Natalie, you never finished telling me what brings you to our city."

"Free airfare." She shrugged. "I told you it wasn't interesting. I have a friend with some frequent flyer miles that were going to expire. So he gave them to me. New Orleans was the most interesting place that the free miles would cover."

"Well, I hope your stay here convinces you that New Orleans is more interesting than many places farther away. What have you got planned?"

"I will cross Bourbon Street off the list tonight, and I have reservations for a class at the New Orleans Cooking School. Is there something else you would recommend?"

"Jazz and food—that's what New Orleans is all about. Don't be discouraged by Bourbon Street. It's becoming more and more of a tourist trap but there are still some places along there that are worth weathering the 'side show.'" Asoph leaned back. "Do you like seafood?"

Nattie nodded.

"For oysters, Acme is the favorite. It's on Iberville, just off Bourbon Street. Felix's is right across the street, though. It's just as good and much less expensive and you can usually get a table right away. Then there's the Red Fish Grill. It's good too, but you better get there before seven."

"Thank you. I'll be sure to check those out." Nattie shifted the topic. "Would you be willing to talk about *The Real McGoo*?"

"Am I willing?" He chuckled. "I just don't know why it took you so long to ask."

"I was a psychology major in college for a while, so I was enthralled with the dialogue between the therapist and the two clients. It held my interest the whole time; but when I got to the end, it dawned on me that all the dialogue was building to the surprise ending."

"Was there a question in there I missed?"

"It just seems to take a lot of skill to hold a reader through all that therapy dialogue to get them to that switch at the end. I mean I never saw it coming." She came very close to adding "and I'm a detective," but

83

asked instead, "It made me wonder, are you a therapist yourself? I mean, the therapy sessions were completely believable."

"Why thank you." Another head bob. "And yes, in my previous life I was a therapist. I take it you did not read the book jacket."

Nattie shook her head.

"*The Real McGoo* did, in fact, grow out of my therapy practice."

"Is that legal? I mean, can you talk about one of your patients like that?"

"Only if I wrote about one particular client. And we don't usually refer to our clients as 'patients'—that's the medical profession's jargon. To be sure, identifying a specific client is illegal and unethical; but as long as no one specifically is identified, then writing about a common issue many people face is fine. So you might say that my Mr. and Mrs. McGoo were not anyone, but they are everyone."

"I found myself really disliking Mr. Tinkers when Mrs. Tinkers described raising the children all alone and not feeling like her husband was invested in anything other than his job."

Asoph nodded.

"And then when you introduced Mr. Evers and he complained about how his wife had frozen him out from the kids. I really came to hate her too."

Asoph rubbed his hands together. "When did that happen?"

"I think it was the chapter when he described feeling emasculated by her in front of their kids. Oh, it really made me mad."

The eyes twinkled. "You wouldn't consider writing a review on Amazon's Web site would you? And my Web site too, if that's not asking too much."

"Of course. Do I just Google your name?" she asked, already knowing the answer.

"That will do it. And thank you. You have really brightened my day. I had the idea for the story when I first started doing marriage counseling forty years ago, but I was worried I could not pull it off. It was a bit tricky to paint each of them sympathetically and then each of their spouses as such villains."

"Well, you pulled it off."

"And you didn't see it coming that they were really married and talking about each other?"

"I didn't. In fact, at one point I remember thinking it was too bad they couldn't find each other."

Asoph's cheeks reddened with delight. "I will tell you the truth, Natalie, I'm sure glad we met today." He slid his chair back from the table. "But now I need to begin my workday."

"Could I take you to dinner?" Nattie blurted out. "I don't want to interfere with your writing, but I would love to talk to you more."

Asoph stood and placed the fingertips of his right hand on his chest. "Alas, it is my misfortune, but you have caught me on one of those rare occasions when I am otherwise engaged."

"Will you be here tomorrow, then?"

"God willing and the creek don't rise." Putting his cap back on, "On the morrow, Ms. Johnson. Enjoy the Cooking School."

CHAPTER 17

KEVIN AND THE DOOR

"Yes, Kevin," she answered the phone through chattering teeth.

"You sound funny. Are you OK?"

Nattie was lying on her bed at the Place D'Armes. Although it was only four in the afternoon she was under the bedspread shivering because she could not figure out how to turn the air-conditioner down. "I'm OK. It's just cold in here."

"The weather channel says it's ninety-six degrees there."

"It is ninety-six degrees here in New Orleans but in my room it's freezing."

"How's it going?"

"So far so good," she told him. "I made contact with Saylor this morning and I'll be meeting him again tomorrow."

"Do you still think you can get what you need without breaking into his office?"

It was a question they had discussed before. Television and movie detectives regularly broke into offices after hours. Nattie had been the teacher's pet in the locksmithing course she took several years ago, but to date she had never needed to resort to those clandestine sorts of tactics. She listened. Listening was her primary skill, followed closely by watching. People talked to her, she was not sure why but they did. For her part she was just curious and interested. It worked and she worked it.

"That's my plan," she answered simply. "How about you, did you fix my back door?"

"That's kinda why I called," he stammered.

"Go on," she said coolly.

"OK. I went to your house this morning. I knew something was weird when I first got inside. I didn't know what it was right away but then it dawned on me. It smelled great in there."

"I know," she told him, "that's the new air freshener I'm using. It's gardenia. I knew it was too sweet for me as soon as I put it out."

"No, sis, that's not it. This was something baking in the oven."

"Eli," she groaned.

"Yeah, it was Eli. He was in the kitchen baking banana nut muffins for you when I walked in. He hid in the closet but I knew he had to be there so I coaxed him out."

"So you met him?"

"I did. He's a nice kid."

"I agree."

"No, I mean it, sis, he's a nice kid."

"What are you saying, Kevin?"

"He's only thirteen years old and he bakes like Ollie. Do you remember him?"

Ollie Ruggiliano was a pastry chef from Chicago who hired Nattie to find his runaway fiancée. Ollie was her first big case and it was to please him that Kevin had given her the name Natasha McMorales because he wanted a detective with a "European sensibility."

"Of course I remember Ollie, but what has that to do with this?"

"I'm just saying the kid can cook and he likes to cook for you."

"Kevin! Did you fix the lock or not?"

"It's fixed as it is."

I'm going to strangle you if you don't answer me. "Did you fix the door so that it would lock?"

"No."

"And I suppose you have a good reason."

"Sure. Everyone knows you don't punch a gift horse in the mouth."

CHAPTER 18

TUESDAY: DAY TWO WITH ASOPH

Nattie had slept well, in spite of the overactive air-conditioner, and so woke early and refreshed, not a common occurrence when she had to travel. Arriving at 7:30 would ensure she had a table near Café Du Monde's back entrance. She did not want to risk another fan to catch Asoph's attention before she got to him this morning.

Arriving at 7:00 would give her enough time to reconnect with the singing bicycle man she had snubbed the day before. His song had stayed with her all the previous day. The lyrics had not registered with her while she heard them, but they had filtered into her awareness throughout the day. The song had something to do with a woman touching the hem of Jesus' robe. If he came back at the same time she planned on recording it with her camera.

There were six people ahead of her when she got in the take-out order line. She assumed the wait would be minimal but several minutes later a huge shopping bag was passed through the window next to the line that declared "Take-Out Only." Apparently that did not just mean coffee and beignets, it also meant gift items for back home. After ten minutes with only two more customers served, Nattie turned to the young man standing behind her and asked, "Is the line always this slow?"

"Everything in New Orleans is slow. You get used to it. It's not like a big city."

Nattie chuckled to herself while she pictured the train stopping across State Street in the "big city" of Bristol, Tennessee. "How long have you been here?"

"Seven years," the young man answered. "I came here from LA, where if you had a flat tire no one would stop. Here, everyone and their grandmother will ask if you're OK."

"Do you mind if I ask you a question?"

"Sure."

"How do people from New Orleans feel about Bourbon Street?"

He rolled his eyes. "That's not New Orleans. There's a lot of history here." He pointed across the street. "There's Decatur and Royal streets." With that he said, "You're up."

"Thanks," she told him. "Have a good day."

The singer was already on the sidewalk and all the tables along the rail were taken by respectful listeners. She had to sit at an interior table for no more than a minute when an elderly couple left one of the tables she hoped to get. She quickly moved to it.

"You want a ringside seat?" the singer smiled, showing no recognition that she had been there the day before.

"I want more than a ringside seat," she told him. "I want to make a request."

"What would you like?"

"I was here yesterday," she confessed, "and I was in a hurry, but you sang a song about Jesus' robe. Would you let me record that?"

The man held out the large wooden cross he wore around his neck. "Certainly, to Him be the glory."

After filming the entire song, Nattie circled through the gate and put a twenty-dollar bill in his bucket. "Thank you, that was wonderful. Did you write that?"

"It's a Sam Cooke song."

"What's your name?" she asked, extending her hand.

"Willie," he told her, as he took her hand.

"Well, to me, it's your song, Willie. That was beautiful."

"Bless you," he said as if he meant it.

The relative peace of the area was suddenly altered when, at ten to eight, twenty servers, all wearing white shirts and little black bow ties appeared in the middle of the room. A short woman, the only one not wearing a paper Café Du Monde hat, began pointing out which server got which area. The chatter factor went sky high as many of the Asian servers translated the directions to each other. And then just as suddenly they were all gone.

"Quite an operation, wouldn't you say, Miss Johnson?" It was Asoph, right on time. He sat down next to her. "How was the Cooking School?"

"It was full," she said with a touch of embarrassment, "and my tickets are for today."

"Was yesterday a Cajun day or a Creole day?" he asked.

"Creole. Today is the Cajun day. Why? What's the different?"

"Okra. Do you like okra?"

Nattie grit her teeth, telling Asoph what he needed to know. "You'll like today better, then. Cajuns don't put okra in their food. There are other differences of course but that's the important one. I see you brought my book."

"Yes. I was hoping you'd autograph it for me."

Asoph took a pen from the pocket of the same shirt he had on the day before. "Authors hate this." As he wrote in her book he asked, "So how did you spend your day?"

"Standard tourist activities. I saw a piano player at the Jazz Historical Center and took their tour. After that, I pretty much walked around. I went to the Rodrique Studios and saw the Blue Dogs. And I found a gelato place."

"La Divina, on St. Peters?"

"Yes."

"Did you try the peach? They make it there themselves from local fruit. I prefer the fragoli, strawberry, but I always ask which is the freshest. Last week it was the peach."

"That sounds good too, but when I read what was in the Azteca chocolate, I couldn't resist."

90

Asoph rolled his hands signaling her to tell him more.

"Cinnamon, honey, and cayenne pepper."

"That sounds terrible."

Nattie smiled. I didn't listen to it, I ate it.

Asoph ordered a black coffee when the server came by.

"Now Natalie, I believe you said there was something else you wanted to discuss."

"I'd like to pick your brain about a story I'm writing myself."

"Ah! A fellow writer. How can I help?"

"I was hoping you could help me with the back story about a character. You know, something psychological that would explain motivation."

"OK. What's the story about?"

"It's about an abused woman, but the character I wanted your input on is a man who comes to her rescue. He is not involved with her in any way, but he goes after her abusive husband."

"Like a knight in shining armor?"

"More like a vigilante. A knight in shining armor would defend her when she was being attacked. In my story the rescuer goes after the abuser in the middle of the night."

"I see."

"So, can you help me give him a background that would make sense?"

Asoph scratched his beard the way one would if he wanted to give the impression he was pretending to think and did not care that it was obvious he was pretending. "Oh, sure," he finally said. "Tell me, is your vigilante violent at other times, or is it only in the defense of women?"

Nattie hesitated while considering the unexpected question. "Just in defense of women, I think."

"First you'd have to give him some inspiration to be a hero. Maybe he could have a father who was a cop who got killed on a domestic violence call or a grandfather who was a volunteer fireman who died saving a child from a burning building."

"Do these men have to be dead?"

Asoph shook his head. "No, they don't have to be dead. They have to have been heroes, however, and then they have to be unavailable."

Nattie must have looked as confused as she felt. Asoph explained, "You see, it is one thing to protect someone you love; protecting someone you don't know is another thing altogether. And if you protect them after the fact—that complicates the equation and requires much more explanation."

Nattie nodded that she was following him.

"Basically he needs to fail."

"Fail? Fail at what?"

"Protecting someone. At a young age he needs to have the responsibility to protect someone placed on him."

"Which is why the heroic father needs to be dead, so the responsibility falls to him."

"Yes." Asoph smiled the smile of a teacher whose pupil just got it right. He noticed another look on Nattie's face. "What are you thinking?"

She raised one eyebrow. "Since you asked, I was wondering about women. Where would a heroic woman fit into the equation? Can women be heroic?"

"Oh mercy, yes. In fact, that would fit the equation very nicely. If the vigilante is a male then he will identify with his male forefathers. And if he is exposed to heroic women as well that will amplify the heroic expectation, but the heroic expectation will come from the gender he identifies with, or to be more exact, the heroic expectation will come from what he believes is expected from that gender."

"Which he could imagine and impose upon himself?"

The teacher's smile returned as he nodded, "Imagine a family of heroes in which the men all die and the women raise our vigilante with their own heroic qualities as well as with tales of his heroic father and grandfather. Now imagine a time when your vigilante was alone with one of his female relatives and something bad happened to her. Picture him too young to have protected her. In fact, it would work better if she got hurt protecting him. It would be a wound he would live with for the rest of his life."

"Are you saying his defense of women would be to make up for what he failed to do as a kid?"

"Or it might be his refusal to live with another failure. Does that work for your story?"

Ignoring his question she asked, "Does the background have to be a wound of some kind? I mean no offense, but does psychology relate everything to a wound or illness?"

92

Asoph's laughter was hearty without being defensive or demeaning. "I think that is a very common belief about us, but I think it better fits the amateurs who read a few self-help books or who took a couple of online courses that emphasize diagnostics."

"But isn't that what you just did—relate the man's action to a wound, I mean?"

"I certainly did include a psychological wound in my explanation, but the wound was not the issue. Compensating for the wound was the issue. All of us have wounds, shortcomings, limitations, and liabilities; but these do not define us. What matters is what we do with it all. It is out of our weaknesses that our strength grows."

"Can't our strengths just be our strengths?"

"Let's see," he said, scooting his chair closer to the table, "what would you say is one of your strengths?"

A surge of nervous energy flooded her. She was uncomfortable having the spotlight pointed at her anytime, but to have it come so unexpectedly really set her on edge. Realizing immediately that he was watching her react did not help her to calm down.

"I'm sorry," he said gently. "I forget what personal questions from a counselor can do. I wouldn't like to be asked to name one of my strengths myself, so let me retract the question."

I think I could trust you, thought Nattie.

"Now, instead of telling me out loud, just think to yourself about a strength or virtue that typifies you. Maybe something someone close to you would say about you."

He waited for her to signal that she had made her choice. In actuality she had decided on two qualities: her sense of responsibility and her care of others. She could not imagine stating either out loud.

"Now," he proceeded, "imagine a time in your life before these qualities took shape. You may have to go back pretty far, but even if you have to go back to your childhood, picture yourself before that strength developed."

Nattie's mind retreated back through her marriage, her college years, her adolescence, and her childhood before she could remember not feeling the weight of responsibility for someone else on her shoulders. The time she finally settled on was when she was four and a half. She was in the living room with her family. Ingrid, her mother, held baby Kevin as she sat on the couch watching Nattie and her father play Twister. The most prevalent part of the memory was the giggling.

"Now," said Asoph, "move forward through your memory to a time when the strength you thought of was fully evident."

The next picture that came to Nattie's memory was when her father was on trial for vehicular manslaughter. Her mother did not want to sit in the courtroom alone, so she took her daughter. Nattie was eight. Nattie flinched as she realized his point.

"I take it that a wound came to mind."

"Does it always work that way?"

"No, but often enough."

"That is very interesting, but do you mind if I change the subject?"

He beckoned to her by extending an open hand, palm up.

"Did you make all that background up or were you thinking of someone who you counseled in the past?"

"As a matter of fact I was thinking of a particular person. But not someone who I counseled."

Nattie felt as if she were on a roller coaster. Her hopes had shot up when Asoph admitted he was speaking of a particular person. Perhaps he had been telling her Beau Robinette's story. But when he added that it was not a former client, they fell out from under her and left her heart hanging in the air.

"He's not living here anymore, but I still keep in touch with him. I could check with him and see if he'd let you interview him if you want. He's living in northeast Tennessee now."

The roller coaster began to climb again. "That would be great. Thank you," she said as she regained her heart.

CHAPTER 19

TUESDAY NIGHT: DAY THREE WITH ASOPH

Nattie had suggested Acme for dinner. Before coming to New Orleans she had been told by several people that Acme was the place to go for oysters. Asoph reminded her of what he had said the day before, Felix's was right across the street, was just as good, and did not include a half-hour wait.

She was sitting at a table facing the door when he walked in at five to six. Waving enthusiastically, he negotiated his way to her table.

"Did you make it to the Cooking School today?" he asked as he took the seat across from her.

"Jambalaya, gumbo, bread pudding, and pray-leans," she answered.

"I see you have been indoctrinated into the correct pronunciation of 'pralines.'"

They each ordered Caesar salads, char-grilled oysters, and sweet potato fries. Asoph ordered a beer.

Nattie asked for sweet tea.

The waitress looked embarrassed. "We don't have sweet tea."

This is the South, isn't it?

"I'm sorry," the waitress continued. "we used to make it but we could never do it right."

But you manage to make oysters three different ways. "That's all right, just water for me."

Although Nattie desperately wanted to know if Asoph's vigilante was Beau, she was determined to wait until Asoph brought the topic up himself. They enjoyed their meal with conversation about favorite authors, movies, and musicians. Because of the nearly thirty years' difference in their ages, author Robert Parker was the only favorite they shared. When they were finished, they ordered coffee.

After the first taste of his coffee, Asoph set his cup down on the table and studied it before lifting his eyes. "I'm sure you have been wondering why I haven't mentioned my phone call to Tennessee."

Nattie could feel her shoulders relax. "I was," she sighed, "but I didn't want to be pushy." I just want to know if it was Beau Robinette.

"First let me say that I have contacted the person we spoke of earlier and he is agreeable to meeting with you."

"Oh good. I was afraid it had not gone well."

"I told him what I have already told you about his story and he has asked that I fill in a few more blanks for you. You see there are some parts of his story that are more embarrassing." Asoph paused and bobbed his head before changing the word, "more painful really. So, Robert has asked me to relate that part of his story."

Nattie's shoulders tensed up again as she heard Asoph say the name.

"Everything I told you about his father and grandfather was true. His father was a policeman who was killed on a domestic disturbance call. That was shortly after Robert's birth."

Pay attention, Nattie told herself, fighting off her disappointment that it was not Beau they were talking about. You're still looking for a vigilante, so all this may still help.

"Robert's mother never remarried. She got a pension from the police department and continued working the family business. Her father, Robert's grandfather, carved walking sticks, which they would sell at craft shows and county fairs. Robert was nine when his grandfather died fighting a fire. So Robert's grandmother, mother, aunt, and older sister banded together to keep the business going as long as the grandfather's supply of carved walking sticks held out." Asoph took another sip of coffee. "That's when Robert came to New Orleans the first time. His other aunt, his mother's younger sister, was supposed to be here studying art so she was given the job of taking care of the young Robert during the summer while the rest of the family could travel from fair to fair."

"She was supposed to be studying art?"

"She was an exotic dancer over on Bourbon Street, only no one in the family knew. She probably did the best she could taking care of a nine-year-old under the circumstances, but it was pretty traumatizing for Robert."

"I can see how."

"Well, it gets worse. It seems the young aunt had a boyfriend, an abusive brute who made a sport of tormenting her. When tempers would flare, Robert would be sent to his room. There he would usually stay put and listen to them call each other names. One night, though, he heard a crash and came rushing out to find his aunt in lying on the couch with the brute on top of her. He was holding her down with a knee on her chest and both hands around her throat."

"Oh my goodness."

"Yes. So what could he do? With the only male role models in his life being heroes who died protecting others, he had no choice."

"What did he do?"

"He jumped on the man's back. Of course, at that age he didn't weigh enough to accomplish anything other than being a distraction. He did succeed in freeing his aunt, but the brute turned his rage on Robert."

Nattie's attention was focused intently on Asoph.

"After slinging Robert to the floor, the attacker produced a knife and began taunting Robert as he slowly walked toward him."

"Obviously he lived," noted Nattie, more to comfort herself than to participate with the story.

"He did. His aunt saw to that. She got between them and sent Robert back to his room with the order that he was to stay there until she came to get him." Asoph stopped speaking and looked solemnly into Nattie's eyes.

She knew the story would not be good. "She never came for him, did she?"

He shook his head. "A neighbor came for him after calling the police. She wrapped him in a blanket so he could not see anything as he passed through the room where his aunt's body lay."

Nattie was silent.

"The next day his mother came and took him home. She tried to tell him that it was not his fault."

"Of course it wasn't his fault," Nattie protested. "Who would blame a nine-year-old for something like that?"

She caught Asoph studying her and realized that he was waiting for her mind to catch up to her voice. "A nine-year-old," she said slowly. "A nine-year-old would blame a nine-year-old for something like that."

"This nine-year-old certainly did."

"And that event could turn a nine-year-old into an adult vigilante?"

"Nothing can make him a vigilante. What happens to us does not determine who we are, but it does provide the material from which we become who we are. It happened and he got to choose how he reacted to it. He could have become a warrior or a pacifist. He could even have become a healer or a lawman. Like I said, he gets to choose how he reacts to it. He just can't choose if he reacts to it."

"Wow." She sighed. "That is quite a story. And a psychology lesson too."

"Well," Asoph's eyes twinkled, "I am what I am."

Didn't Popeye say that? Nattie remembered the expression from the Cartoon Network. "Anything else?"

"Yes, as a matter of fact, there is. I picked the name Robert because of our mutual affection for Robert Parker, but Robert is not his name."

She felt the roller coaster begin to climb again, "What is his name then?"

"I think you already know, don't you, Natasha?"

CHAPTER 20

NO FOOD

"Kevin?" Nattie called out from her office when she heard the door open. It was Thursday morning. Her business in New Orleans, having been settled on Tuesday evening, gave her all day on Wednesday to travel home and envision this conversation with her office manager.

"Hey, Sarge!" he said over his shoulder as he swung his backpack off and onto his desk. "How was N'awlins? Tell me everything."

She waited until he entered her office and stood before her desk. Then in her best schoolteacher voice she asked, "Did you, by chance, happen to mention to anyone about my trip to New Orleans?"

Sensing that he might be in trouble he stepped back. "Me? No, I didn't say anything to anyone. Why?" He plopped down on one of the upholstered chairs in front of her desk, "What happened?"

"Are you absolutely sure you spoke to no one? No one at all?"

"Really, Nattie, no one. I just got information about New Orleans for your trip, but that's all."

"That's all?"

"Yeah, why?"

"You told me you found Place D'Armes online."

"I did. But then I found some more information for you."

"What information about New Orleans did you get for me and where did you get it?" *It's Beau, isn't it? I know it's Beau, you pinhead!*

"Come on, Nat. What's going on? Everything I got I told you about before you left."

"Kevin," she said harshly, "you did not tell me any such thing."

"I sent you an e-mail. I know I did." He stood and spread his arms. "Let's go look."

"Look, Kevin, this is serious. You have got to be careful about any information regarding a client or an investigation I'm on. It could cost me my license."

"Do you think I don't know that? If you think I have shared information about you, then tell me now what you're accusing me of."

"OK, Kevin, did you get your information from Beau Robinette?"

"Of course," he answered with a confused look on his face. "Beau is the one who gave me all the information about that author."

"Well, Kevin, here's the problem. Beau Robinette is my prime suspect. If he knows that I was in New Orleans talking to Asoph Saylor, then he knows that I was checking up on him. You see why that's a problem, don't you?"

"How was I supposed to know that?"

"You're not supposed to know who is a suspect and who is not. That's why you're not supposed to let anyone know what I'm doing."

Kevin raised his eyebrows. "I'm not sure what happened down there, but in the past you always told me to let the client know where you were, but not what you were doing. Has that changed?"

Nattie's face grew flushed with embarrassment. "Oh, Kevin, I'm so sorry. I was upset with you because Beau knew I was there and I completely forgot that he is the client too. Please forgive me. This is all my fault."

Staggering back down into his chair, Kevin made the whistle sounds of a bomb dropping. "Wow! That's a real mind bender. The client is the suspect. He could have saved us a lot of time if he just came in and hired us to find him while he was still in the office." He chortled. "Why hire us if he's guilty?"

"I don't know."

"Is he guilty?"

"I don't know that either, but I'm going to find out." She stood up and extended her arm. "And you are going to help me."

Kevin took her outstretched hand. "At your service, Sarge. What do you need?"

"First, I need you to forgive me."

He brushed the request off with his hand. "No need for that. You had a good reason to be angry. It was an easy misunderstanding, and now we're all good."

"Thank you. I wasn't angry, though; I was upset."

"In our family, being upset is code for angry."

He was right and she knew it. But saying it out loud was breaking the rules, which is what he always did. Her response was to proceed, which was what she always did.

"I want you to do your computer magic and find out everything you can about Frank Lester and Beau Robinette."

Kevin put his thumb up and winked. "No problem. Is there anything in particular you're looking for?"

"With Beau I want you to find out everything you can about his stint with the Washington County Sheriff's office. I especially want to know about the case he was involved in that ended his time there. Apparently he beat up an abusive man and decided to leave town rather than face an investigation. I want to know what about that is fact and what is fiction."

"And Lester?"

"He's a slug. I'm guessing there is a long list of people who are glad he got clubbed, but I want to know if there are any of those glad folks who might have done it. Check with Detective Henry Quayle."

"Done. Anything else?"

"Not at the moment, but don't go too far." In a timid voice, she asked, "Are we OK?"

"We are," he said, "if you tell me your top-five list from New Orleans."

"How do you know I have a top-five list?"

He bowed his head and peered at her over a pair of glasses that were not there.

"OK, number one has to be Café Du Monde."

Kevin nodded, "Chicory coffee and beignets."

"Have you been there?"

"No," answered Kevin, "but it's on my bucket list."

"How do you know about Café Du Monde?"

"It was the first thing on Beau's list too."

"Did he mention Willie?"

Kevin shook his head.

"Willie is a street performer. He comes by the café around seven o'clock in the morning and sings to anyone sitting near the sidewalk. He does a version of a Sam Cooke song about the woman who touches the hem of Jesus' robe that will make you cry."

"Number two?"

"Number two is the Saint Louis Basilica off Jackson Square. It's a little like the old churches I saw in Tuscany with artwork all over the place. There's even a big painting of Saint Francis."

"Are you getting religious on us?"

Nattie ignored his question. "I was there on Pentecost Sunday and they did some kind of confirmation service with 137 adults. It was pretty interesting."

"Did you go to the service?"

"I did. It was OK. I knew when to stand but I didn't know when to kneel. It didn't seem to bother anyone, though. Was that on Beau's list?"

"I don't think so," said Kevin, "but Bourbon Street was."

"My next two are on Bourbon Street. First was a jazz club in the Hotel Royal Sonesta. I went there on Monday night because I heard about Bob French and the Original Tuxedo Jazz Band. They only play there on Monday nights, and there's a bass player named Richard Moulton who did things with that bass that I have never seen before."

"You should start a blog of the places you go and what to do there."

"You mean what I eat there."

"You'd include that too, of course. You do have a nose for interesting places."

"That's why I look the way I do."

"Can I have a dollar?"

She fished a dollar out of her pocket and handed it to him, "What do you want a dollar for?"

"Christmas party."

"Give me the dollar back," she said, rolling her eyes.

102

Holding the dollar in his left hand, Kevin lifted his right index finger. "I'm going to collect a dollar from you every time you take a shot at yourself. I'll put it in a savings account and we'll do something at Christmas."

She squinted at him. "What if I just think it?"

"You'll have to police that yourself."

"And if I think something about you?"

Kevin waved his right hand in dismissal. "You couldn't afford that."

"Keep the dollar."

While he stuffed the dollar in his shirt pocket, she continued with her list. "After the jazz performance, I walked back down Bourbon Street and when I got to Orleans, which is just before Anne Street where the Place D'Armes is, I saw an amazing sight. St. Louis Basilica is about three stories high and is mostly white with very few windows on the side. It's about two blocks from Bourbon Street and there is a lit-up statue of Jesus on the edge of the lawn facing Bourbon Street."

"So anyone who looks down that street can see Jesus watching them do what they are doing there?"

"And there's a three-story shadow backing him up."

"OK, this is weird. You have three religious things on your list and no food. What gives?"

"Number five is food. It's the New Orleans Cooking School."

"I remember getting you the tickets."

"Was that on Beau's list?"

"It was."

"So what else is on his list?"

"He talked about a New Orleans Jazz National Historical Park where they do free concerts every day. Then there's Central Grocery where they invented the muffaletta sandwich. He said they were across the street from each other and about a block away from Café Du Monde."

"I wish I had gotten your e-mail. Are you sure you sent it?"

"Absolutely. I put NEW ORLEANS FOOD on the subject line to make sure you'd look at it."

Swinging around ninety degrees to face her computer, Nattie opened her e-mail. "I know why I didn't see his list," she observed, pointing at the screen.

"What?" he asked with a well-conditioned innocence.

"You didn't put NEW ORLEANS FOOD in the subject line, you put NO FOOD."

CHAPTER 21

THURSDAY: MEETING WITH BEAU

"You met my friend Asoph Saylor. How is he?" Beau stood next to the booth where Nattie sat. She had asked for a meeting, but insisted it be away from Nathan's tavern, the Our House. Beau had picked Machiavelli's, which meant all she had to do was cross the parking lot.

"He seemed fine to me." She pointed at the bench across from her. "Do you come here very often?"

He scanned the dining room. It was dimly lit, with dark wood floors and walls of exposed brick lined with artwork. "No, but it's nice in here. I like the music. Is that Alison Kraus?"

"I think so. Please, sit."

As he slid into the booth across from her, the waitress appeared with two waters, "Do you know what you want?"

"I'll have the Greek salad," ordered Nattie, "but he may need a few minutes."

"No, I can order now." He ran his finger down the left side of the menu. "I'll try the Italian nachos, and bring me the glazed pears for dessert." After handing her his menu he noticed the Fat Tire beer advertisement on the table. "And I'll take one of these too."

As soon as the waitress was gone, he patted his stomach, "This is the first time I've been in here, but I looked up their menu online. It's a great menu." Then his face changed as if he just happened to think of something. "Say, speaking of great menus, how did you like New Orleans?"

Determined not to let him set a chatty tone to their conversation, she frowned. "Tell me, Beau, you knew I was going to New Orleans before I left, didn't you?"

He nodded, but otherwise showed no reaction to her statement. Instead, he seemed to study her. I have to remember he's a trained counselor, she reminded herself.

"Did you know that you were the suspect I was following up on?"

"Of course. I'm Henry Quayle's primary suspect. Actually, I'm afraid I'm his only suspect, so I knew he'd point you toward me. And I knew what he'd probably tell you about my leaving Washington County."

"So you know what this conversation has to be about too, don't you?"

"I do."

"Then I don't understand. Why didn't you just start with this conversation and save all the expense of me going to New Orleans? That will be part of my bill to you, you know?"

"I know, but if I had told you all that stuff, you would still have to ask me if I attacked Frank Lester, wouldn't you?"

Nattie nodded.

"If we'd have talked first, then my credibility would have been a bigger issue and the time in New Orleans would have taken longer. So this was cheaper in the long run. I know I'm a suspect—that doesn't bother me—but I want to know that other suspects are being looked into as well. Frank Lester is a bad guy and that means there are probably lots of people with reasons to attack him. I want to know someone is checking all of them out, not just me."

"So that's why you hired me. To make sure I'd check them all out, including you."

"Yep."

"Well, let me cut right to the chase, then. Did you attack Frank Lester?"

106

Beau laughed. "That was right to it." Then composing himself, he looked right at her and said, "Of course I am going to deny it. I did not even know him when he got attacked. That was before I started working at the Our House. What you are finding in my history is evidence that I am capable of doing it, but even that is faulty."

Nattie studied him.

"Look, Natasha, Quayle is looking for a vigilante and he thinks I'm a vigilante, right?"

"As far as I know that's right."

"And you have followed that lead to see if I fit the profile for a vigilante, right?"

"Yes."

"And I do, right?"

"As far as I understand it, yes."

"But am I?"

"Are you?"

"Am I a vigilante? Have I ever done anything vigilante like?"

Nattie could not help but look confused. His reasoning was flawless so far; but he was moving quickly, so her instinct was to slow down rather than agree.

"Why don't you ask me the questions about my history that you don't have answers to yet."

"OK," she agreed, "tell me about your return to New Orleans. When you left Washington County why did you go back to New Orleans?"

The question was not the one he had expected so it took a moment to answer. "I suppose it was because it was the only other place I'd ever known."

"Did you try to find the man who had murdered your aunt?"

"No."

Nattie took a long breath.

"You don't believe me, do you?"

They locked eyes for a long moment before she answered, "No, I don't."

"What if I told you that long before I returned to New Orleans I knew he was dead? Would you believe that I followed the one parole hearing he was granted before he died? Would you believe that I did have fantasies of beating him to death with my hands, but they never came to pass?"

"I'll believe all that when I verify the dates. And I will verify the dates."

He bowed. "I would expect nothing less."

"What about your resignation from Washington County?"

"Do you want to hear the story of how I came to be accused of breaking Gray Rankin's jaw?"

"That is the story that has vigilante written all over it."

"Only if you don't have all the facts."

"I'm listening," she said.

"Gray Rankin was an old coot with a thirty-six-year-old wife and two teenage daughters."

"She was a young mom."

"Eighteen when she had her first and another right away. It would have been a tough parenting job under any circumstances, but she was also young and inexperienced. Old man Rankin was no help. I was the juvenile officer so the family fell into my lap when the girls started getting into trouble. It was nothing real bad: running away, underage drinking, and I think shoplifting once with the younger girl. Anyway, I started working with the family and it became very clear very fast that they needed counseling. So I encouraged Mrs. Rankin to get help."

Nattie could not help wondering if Mrs. Rankin had fallen in love with her hero.

"I guess she didn't put much hope in counseling helping, because she went home and asked Rankin for a divorce. The next time I went to their house, he got in my car and shoved a three-inch pocketknife up against my thigh. He drew a little blood, but we just sat like that while he blamed me for taking his wife and kids from him. He vented for about five or six minutes and I listened. I thought it was going well until I said he might be able to save his family if he went to counseling. That's when he screamed like a wolf and shoved that knife all the way in, down to the bone."

"Oh my."

"I don't know what I was thinking, my hands were up on the steering wheel, and when that knife went in me I freaked out. I hit that man with a backhand that had all my strength and what I'm sure was an adrenalin overload in it."

She looked at him again. He had always looked like a gentle giant to her, but now he looked different. He was not just big. "So you did shatter his jaw."

"I did," Beau admitted. "But I did not go looking for him. He came looking for me."

"OK, that seems innocent enough. Why leave?"

"It was time to go. I'd been putting it off, but what I wanted to be was a counselor and that meant going back to school. Staying would have meant an investigation that would have ended badly for Gray Rankin, and that would not have done anyone any good."

"Why do you say that? He stabbed you. What did he do to his family?"

"Well he and I had a heart-to-heart before I left and he agreed to let her move out as long as she agreed to meet with a social worker. The threat of my returning to prosecute him was enough to keep his nose clean."

"Did it work?"

"Yes and no. They ended up divorcing, but he kept his nose clean."

"I don't suppose you can verify that, can you?"

"As a matter of fact, I can forward you the last report I got from the social worker."

"You can?" Nattie was surprised. "I thought that would violate confidentiality or something."

"The social worker is OK because the Rankins signed a release so I could keep tabs on him."

"What about you? Can you violate his confidentiality?"

"It's not an issue for me. I don't have a license anymore."

"What's that story?"

"Well, after I got my degree from Tulane I was in practice with Asoph in the French Quarter. I worked with a woman whose husband was an abusive SOB." His face lit up, "Hey, there's a time I could have been a vigilante, and I wasn't."

"How did it cost you your license, then?"

That was the moment their food came to the table. The Greek salad was unusual in that everything in it was cut into half-inch cubes. But it was very large and tasted very Greek.

Beau offered her some of his Italian nachos. She declined. Beau took such a huge mouthful that his lips looked like he was kissing air when he chewed. After wiping the Alfredo sauce from his mouth and taking a long draft of his beer, he leaned forward and confessed, "I had an affair with her." He sat back and shrugged. "I said I wasn't a vigilante. I never said I was an angel."

CHAPTER 22

KEVIN'S RESEARCH

Nattie was sitting along the rail in the balcony of the Blackbird Bakery rereading *The Real McGoo* by Asoph Saylor when Kevin sat down with a large cup of coffee and a Key lime bar. "Do you want a bite?"

"No thanks. What did you find out for me?"

His mouth was puckered from the tartness of the Key lime. He waved a finger across his face signaling for her to wait. After swallowing hard, he said, "I'm fine, thank you. As a matter of fact, I'm having a great day." He cut another fork full of Key lime bar and, using it as a baton, added, "You need to learn how to relax."

She had been told that before. It always had the same effect: the tightening of the muscles in the back of her neck, followed by the temptation to toss some flavor of pie into the face of whoever offered the unsolicited advice. If she were especially irritated, it would be a blueberry pie she pictured tossing. "What makes this a great day?" she asked with syrupy enthusiasm.

By this time he had another bite in his mouth and another loaded on his fork. He waved toward the front of the bakery with the fork while he savored the bite in his mouth. "Do you see those girls?" he finally asked.

It was nine in the morning, so the bakery was full of women. There was, however, no mistaking which "girls" he was referring to. Although they were seated at one of the outside tables, Nattie could tell that each one was six feet tall or better, and each had long legs, willowy arms, and sassy European haircuts. The blonde on the left sported an expensive pair of sunglasses on top of her head, while the redhead on the right had on glasses with dark red frames that should have clashed with her hair. "What about them?" she asked.

"They gave me a nine."

"I'm sorry?"

"As I walked by, I heard them rate me."

"And they gave you a nine?"

He grinned. "Both of them."

Nattie looked again at the two swimsuit models on the sidewalk. "Those women," she repeated. These women were tens, maybe elevens. Then she turned toward Kevin, who had a large dollop of green filling on his cheek and a smattering of powered sugar across his black T-shirt. "They gave you a nine."

"It makes you see me in a new light, doesn't it?"

"Not at all, Kevin. But if you're planning on connecting with one of those women, you might want to clean up a little bit."

He looked down and immediately began brushing himself off. This had the effect of not only streaking the powered sugar farther down his chest, but of also dislodging the Key lime filling, which landed directly in the middle of his zipper flap.

Oh you're a nine all right, she thought.

"Oh well," he finally said, scooping up the pudding with his finger and putting it in his mouth, "easy come, easy go."

"Their loss, Kev," Nattie said softly.

He did not hear her. His attention was already redirected toward his next bite of Key lime bar, which he savored with his eyes closed.

You really are a nine, she thought, marveling at how rapidly he had maneuvered from a disappointment to a celebration.

He finished the last bite, put down the fork, and after wetting his finger dabbed up the powdered sugar remnant.

"Do you want to go ahead and just lick the plate? They're not looking."

112

Kevin held up the plate so the women on the sidewalk could see it if they were looking and slowly dragged his tongue across it.

Nattie held both her hands out as if introducing him to the universe. "My brother, the nine."

He bowed ceremoniously; and when he came up, he was holding his messenger bag. "Do you want to see what I found out?"

"I thought you'd never ask. Did you find me any good candidates who might have attacked Frank Lester?"

"You're going to like this." He took a manila folder from his bag and slid it across the table. As Nattie picked it up, he placed his hand on top of it. "Let me tell you a few things before you look at that."

"OK," she said retracting her hand.

"I could divide the information on him into three categories. The first is that there have been a few complaints about him in the last five or six years, but nothing more than what Detective Quayle already gave you."

"No convictions."

"None," confirmed Kevin. "Then there's the second category—his military career. He's a helicopter pilot and has done two tours of duty in the Middle East. He was awarded several commendations and got lots of press."

"Is he a hero?"

"He's definitely a risk taker. And he has done some heroic things."

"But—" She prodded him to get to the point.

"There's no question he is talented, but he's a self-serving bully too. Let me tell you about the rest of the information on him. He was a pretty good athlete. A left-handed pitcher with a blazing fastball and something most left-handed fastball pitchers don't have."

"What's that?"

"Control. There are newspaper articles about him going back to his Little League days. He led his high school team to the Virginia State finals. They lost that game 1 to 0 in the last inning; but by all accounts, he pitched a phenomenal game, striking out twelve and walking two."

"Impressive."

"Yes. Then he went to college on a baseball scholarship. Jefferson International University. Have you ever heard of it?"

She shook her head.

"It's an NCAA Division II school in Southwest Virginia. The fact that it's right near here and you've never heard of it tells you how big it is. Anyway he started out in the bullpen, but made the starting rotation by the end of his freshman year. As a sophomore he was the ace of the staff and was leading the nation in strikeouts when it all unraveled on him."

Sitting back, Kevin motioned that it was time for Nattie to open the folder, which she did. Inside were three sheets of paper. The first page was a copy of a newspaper article titled "Hammerin' Hank Gets Clutch Hit." It was a write-up of the Virginia State High School finals in which Frankie Lester gave up a fluke hit to someone named Hammerin' Hank after Henry Aaron.

Holding the page up, she asked, "Is this the game you were telling me about?"

"It is."

"Can you give me the highlights?"

"Sure. Like I said, Frankie Lester pitched a phenomenal game. It was a zero-to-zero tie going into the ninth inning when a two-base error put a runner in scoring position with nobody out. Frankie struck out the next two batters on six pitches, which brought the other team's shortstop to the plate. Now the shortstop was a pretty good defensive player, and he would get a baseball scholarship too, but he wasn't a hitter. He had been at the plate twice already and struck out once and fouled out once."

"And he got a bloop hit," guessed Nattie.

"Nope. He got the hit of his life. A line-drive double between the left and center fielders. Game over."

"Well, that sets the stage for Lester to have a grudge against Hank, but not the other way."

"You're getting ahead of the story, sis."

"Fair enough," she said. "What is it that you want me to get in this story?"

"Did you notice what Hank's last name is?"

Nattie returned to the page and scanned down until she found what she was looking for. "Quayle!" she exclaimed. "Hank, the shortstop, is Henry Quayle?"

"It's an interesting coincidence, isn't it?"

"I'll say."

114

"And the coincidences keep on coming because these two high-school rivals end up at rival colleges a year later."

"Really," she said, half under her breath as she looked at the second piece of paper. This page was a copy of an article about how Hank Quayle had been hit in the head by a fastball thrown by Frank Lester. The hit resulted in a concussion for Henry Quayle and ended his baseball career. According to the sports writer, Frank Lester was a "headhunter," who went after his high-school rival. Frank was quoted as saying that he did not know he was facing the same shortstop from high school and that pitching high and inside is just part of the sport that occasionally has unfortunate results.

The last page was a copy of an article titled "Quayle Hunting Backfires." Apparently, during the week preceding the game in which Henry Quayle was hurt, Frank Lester invited several classmates to come to the game and watch as he went "Quayle Hunting." The NCAA banned Frank Lester for life, stating that his transgression was both vicious and premeditated.

"Wow," she said as she closed the folder on the table.

"Do you think Quayle beat up Lester to get even?" Kevin asked.

"He certainly had motive and he didn't disclose his history with Frankie. At least he didn't disclose it to me." Nattie thought a moment. "You know, he's not really been open to consider any other suspects besides Beau. This could be why."

"So you do think he did it?"

Nattie stood to leave. "I think I need to find out." She patted her brother on the shoulder as she waked by. "Thanks, Kevin; this is good."

Her departure took Nattie right by the outside table where the two leggy swimsuit models still sat. They were too deep in their conversation to notice her slowing down to listen to them. She had no idea what they were saying, but it was clear they were speaking German.

CHAPTER 23

NATTIE CONFRONTS HENRY

"Ms. McMorales," he said standing over her.

Nattie looked up from her copy of *Still Life* by Louise Penny. "Why, Detective Quayle, what brings you here?"

He spread his arms as if to say, "Is it not obvious?" "This is a coffee shop. I come here every morning. For coffee." He leaned forward to look into her cup. "Do you need a refill?"

She, of course, knew why he was there. It was a rare morning that he did not wander into Zazzy'z Coffee House between 8:30 and 9:00. She was waiting for him. "Not quite yet, thanks, but after you order, please come join me."

"I will. I'm eager to hear how your investigation is going."

"And I am eager to hear about yours as well." And, Hammerin' Hank, I'm especially eager to hear about your history with Frankie Lester.

Henry Quayle returned to the table with a travel mug decorated with Zazzy'z label and with another mug full of coffee, "I usually have them do a refill with this," he said, holding up the travel mug. "It's cheaper that way; but if I'm going to sit here with you for a while, it works out better to use their mug."

"Because of the free refills." Nattie stated the obvious.

"You see," he explained, "using their mug costs a little more but they don't charge you for the refills."

"I'll have to remember that."

"You know," he said, lifting his mug, "coffee has become very trendy these days. That's why coffee shops emphasize different degrees of darkness and how fresh the roasting was, but I don't think many people can really tell the difference."

"I don't know that," she countered. "I know I can tell if the coffee is too weak and watery."

"But can you tell if the bean came from Uganda or Colombia?"

"Probably not, but I'm sure some people can."

"Me too, but I'm saying the number of people who can tell the difference is much smaller than the number of people who think they can. And those people are wasting their money on something that doesn't matter."

Why do you care how they spend their money?

"It's like the people who buy the more expensive gas even though their car doesn't use the additives the more expensive gas has. It's just vanity."

"It's a good thing that we don't that problem." Nattie felt a pang of guilt when she noticed him flinch at the sarcasm she had been sure he would not catch.

"I had some great coffee in New Orleans," she said trying to move away from the awkward moment.

"That's right, New Orleans," he said, having already recovered from her remark. "So you got to follow up on the lead I gave you."

"I did. I spent almost four days in the French Quarter, a fair amount of that time with the therapist who knew Mr. Robinette."

"Oh good. Tell me what you found out. Is Beau Robinette a vigilante?"

"As I said, I got to talk to Mr. Saylor, or maybe it's Dr. Saylor; I never asked about that. Anyway, he seemed to know a lot about the psychological factors that might go together to shape a vigilante."

"And?" Henry asked impatiently.

"And there is no doubt that Mr. Robinette fits that profile to a tee."

Henry clapped his hands together. "I knew it."

"But!" Nattie responded, more abruptly than she meant. Henry Quayle's refusal to grant others the consideration he himself expected was a growing source of irritation she would need to stay on top of. "According to Dr. Saylor, fitting the profile does not mean that he is a vigilante. That profile could have shaped him into being a healer, like the good doctor. And it could have shaped him into being a protector, like you, Detective."

Henry tapped his finger on the table. "Yes, but the lawmen that fit that profile usually end up going too far, exposing their true character." Pointing at Nattie, he added, "And that's what happened to your buddy, Beau." He sat back. "So tell me, what did you find out about his background that fits the profile?"

The question felt surprisingly intrusive to her. She was not convinced Beau was innocent, but her instinct was to protect him. The personal information she had about his history was information he had given to her. At least he knowingly allowed her to obtain it. Henry Quayle was not entitled to it. "The usual stuff, a hero father who cast a long shadow and left bigger-than-life shoes to fill," she answered, giving Quayle only what she was sure he already knew. "But there are things that do not fit too."

"Like what?" the detective asked, sounding authentically interested.

"Well, if the vigilante stuff was an uncontrollable compulsion, there would have been a history of possibly lesser, but similar acts."

Henry shook his head, "What do you call that incident that ended his police career?"

"You tell me. My understanding is that he was not charged with anything in that incident."

"He could have cut a deal to resign instead of face prosecution."

"Do you know anything that indicates a deal was made?"

"No, but I wouldn't."

Right, because there is no grapevine in police departments. "So that's conjecture."

He rolled his eyes.

"OK, tell me what you do know. In Mr. Robinette's account, he was in his car and the other man got in. Does that fit your understanding?"

"Yes, but Robinette could have picked him up."

"And is it also accurate that Mr. Robinette was provoked?"

"I'm sure that is his story."

"He was stabbed in the thigh."

"Yes, but was he stabbed before or after he threw his punch? He shattered that man's jaw. Do you have any idea how much force that would take?"

"More force than I possess, I'm sure, but let me ask you about that injury. Was that jaw broken by one hit or several?"

"I don't know. What difference does it make?"

"A single blow would support the claim that it was a defensive act."

"At least it would not contradict the claim that it was defensive. It doesn't prove it, though."

"No, that is true; but that brings us to the simple question of which is the more credible story."

"And I don't think Beau's story is credible."

"Let me review. The evidence that he attacked Frank Lester is that he fits a profile of a vigilante."

"That is a gross oversimplification."

"Maybe so, but please allow me to present my whole review, and then you can add or subtract."

"Go ahead counselor," he said sarcastically.

"Thank you. So the key to the vigilante theory is the incident in which he broke that man's jaw. Agreed?"

"So far."

"And we don't know whether Mr. Robinette picked him up or he got into the car uninvited. Agreed?"

"Agreed."

"Now we come to the key fact, whether the hit or the stab came first. Agreed?"

Henry shrugged.

"I'll admit that the hitting could have come before or after the stabbing," she offered by way of appeasing the detective.

Henry patted his hand on the table. "Well thank you for that."

"And of course the stabbing could have come before the hitting. However, can you honestly tell me that an old man could have gathered himself together enough to stab someone in the thigh after his jaw was, as you say, shattered?"

Henry Quayle huffed.

"I don't know what kind of pain he was in, but I'm guessing if he miraculously stayed conscious at all, the most he could do was collapse."

"You present a good argument. Beau is getting his money's worth."

"If I find out he's guilty, he won't think so."

"Are you really open to that possibility, Ms. McMorales?"

"I am. Are you open to the possibility that someone else is guilty?"

"Of course," he answered indignantly.

"Really? Then let me ask you how many other suspects have you considered?"

"I can't give you those kinds of details." Henry's retort was in a higher pitch than normal.

"I didn't ask for any details that would compromise your investigation. I asked for a number. It was a simple straightforward question and you balked."

"What are you accusing me of?"

"I'm accusing you of running a shortsighted investigation."

"And why are you suggesting I would do that?" Henry spoke loudly enough for other patrons in the coffee house to turn and stare.

"I don't know, Detective. Why don't you tell me why you withheld your history with Frank Lester? He gave you a concussion, didn't he?"

Henry stood up quickly, knocking his chair over. "This conversation is over." In an attempt to make his way out, he stumbled over his fallen chair. He righted himself, took a slow deep breath, and, without looking back, left. Both his coffee mugs remained on the table.

CHAPTER 24

SURPRISE AT ZAZZY'Z

"Are you in a hurry?"

Nattie jumped. The sound of his voice startled her. She had been watching Henry's short choppy walk to his car so she had not seen Nathan approach her table. "Nathan! What are you doing here?"

"I came to see you, Nat. Can I sit down?"

"How did you know I was here?"

"Kevin told me you were meeting someone at nine o'clock." He glanced at his watch. "It's nine thirty. Do you have a few minutes?"

She was slow to answer. "I'm sorry. Just changing gears. Please, sit down."

"Just a second," he said before retrieving his coffee mug from the tall table where he had been waiting.

"Did you want to talk about the case?" she asked as he sat down next to her.

Shaking his head, he put a small flat package on the table. "I found this," he told her. It was wrapped in pages from the Sunday comic strips.

"Is this a book?" she guessed holding it up.

"You're the detective." He smiled.

Tearing the flap at one end of the package, she slid a small frame from inside. "Oh my goodness!" She picked it up and held it against her heart. "Where did you find this?"

"It was in that Georgia O'Keefe art book you gave me for our paper anniversary."

"And you had it framed."

"It was your grandfather's blessing at our wedding. It makes sense that you should have it. I just wanted to make it nice."

"Thank you," she said, softly resting her hand on his forearm. "I had given this up for lost."

She did not notice him blush, or his eyes dilate, or feel him rotate his arm toward her touch as she read the poem aloud.

A WEDDING BLESSING

The time has come, the walrus said
To speak of many things
Of Nattie's dress and Nathan's vest
And the exchange of wedding rings.

To each other may you always speak,
Lovingly, faithfully, and truthfully.
For love endures and faith sustains
And the Truth will set you free.

That you each may mature
Into the completeness of God's intent
As you gain wisdom, joy, and perseverance
From every trial, whenever it is sent.

Thru thick and thin may you always rejoice,
And find rest in the Father's hands.
And may your children know the shepherd's voice,
And may they all become Cub fans.

The Wolf

A single tear appeared at the edge of her eye when she finished. "I can still see the Wolf as he read this to us." William Johnson was "Grand Wolf" to his grandchildren when he was present, but they always referred to him as "the Wolf" when he was not. After he died Kevin threatened to chisel "the Wolf" on his headstone if they did not include it. It was an unnecessary threat. Wiping away the tear, she withdrew her hand from his forearm without noticing he had placed his left hand alongside hers.

"This is very nice, Nathan. Thank you again. The frame is beautiful. I'm not sure where, but I will find a place of honor for it." Putting it back into the paper wrapper and stowing it in her shoulder bag, she added, "But you didn't have to make a special trip all the way up here."

"I wanted to. I have good memories about this place from when we were married."

"Me too."

"Say, do you remember that author we met here?"

"Do you mean Delia Davenport?"

"Yes. And I got her to sign her cookbook for you, remember?"

"Of course. I still use that book." Her encounter with Eli Anderson and her rediscovery of the slug flashed though her thoughts. She reached down and felt her pocket. There the slug rested against her leg. She desperately wanted him to recall that part of the story, but hoped he would not at the same time. "I remember that day very well," *Do you?* "It was a very good day for us," *But was it real?* Without realizing it, she gave him no time to respond before shifting the conversation. "I understand you have a big celebration at Our House tonight."

"We do. You should come by. In a way you are the honored guest."

"You mean my old BlackBerry phone is."

"Well, it was your phone."

Nattie scowled. "Did he tell people it was my phone?"

Nathan put his hands up defensively. "Calm down. Kevin did it the way you wanted him to."

"He told them it was his phone?"

"He did. He put your top five reasons for destroying your BlackBerry on the chalkboard, but he said they were his reasons."

"And how many raffle tickets did he sell for the right to destroy it?"

"Close to eighty, I think."

"Eighty? That's incredible!"

"I think he could have gotten more if he had waited longer."

She smiled and shook her head. "You have to admit, he knows how to work the angles. How much did he charge for each ticket?"

"Five bucks."

"Five bucks," she repeated then, looking toward the ceiling, did the math, "That's four hundred dollars!"

"I know."

"Four hundred dollars is more than I paid for my new iPhone!"

"You have to admit—" Nathan paused to grin. "He knows how to work the angles."

Nattie laughed gently.

"You should come tonight," Nathan continued. "He's going to draw a name out of the hat at eight o'clock."

"I don't know." *Why don't you ask me out to dinner?*

"I bought a ticket for you. You could get the honors."

"I could have had the honors while I still owned the stupid thing."

"This will be much more fun, though. I'd like you to come. That is, if you're not working or something else."

"If eighty people are going to be there, isn't that going to put you over the fire code limit?"

"It will probably be more like thirty. Some people won't show, and lots of people bought more than one ticket. It will be fun."

She looked at him, "Will Randi Lester be there?" she asked in a lower voice.

"No. That's over."

"I'm glad," she said. "I think you need to be very, very careful with Frank Lester, Nathan." *Did you give her the slug story, too? Or do you even remember telling it to me?*

In a soft voice he asked, "Is that the only reason you don't want her to be there?"

Avoiding eye contact with him, she looked at her watch. It was almost ten o'clock. She had nowhere to get to, but said, "Oh my, I've lost track of the time. I'm sorry, I have to run."

She stood up quickly to return her mug and Henry Quayle's to the side bar. Then she took Henry's travel mug to the counter and explained to Sammi that he had forgotten it. All the while, Nathan sat staring at his own coffee mug.

"Thank you," she said, touching his shoulder. "I don't think I can make it, but I appreciate the invitation."

He nodded silently.

Turning back as she opened the door, she added, "And thanks again for the Wolf's poem."

He smiled and nodded at her as she waved good-bye. She could not see that under the table he was rubbing his thumb across another slug, making another wish.

CHAPTER 25

BLACK SATURDAY

It was five to eight when Nattie entered Our House. There may not have been eighty people, but it was far more crowded than the thirty Nathan said he expected. She recognized none of the customers milling around at that end of the bar.

The chalkboard to the right of the front entrance bore the top five ways her Smartphone had outsmarted her:

It cannot be touched anywhere without triggering something.

It reboots itself whenever the opportunity to take a picture is fleeting.

When it went through an "upgrade" half of the photos disappeared.

You cannot tell what letter you are touching on the touch screen because even though the letter lights up when you touch it, you can't see the light through your finger.

Unwanted APPs run advertising at random and must be figured out before they can be turned off.

At the bottom it was signed, "An unknown user of limited computer comfort."

126

Nattie did not need to have the conversation with Kevin to know what he would say. She'd ask, "Why didn't you sign your name like you agreed to. People will know that I'm the user with limited computer comfort." And he would respond, "No one would believe I made those user mistakes, so they'd think it's you anyway." Then she'd say, "They still think it's me." And to that he would say, "Anyone who knows us will think it's you at first, but they'd assume I'd use your name if it was you so they'll think it's someone else this way." *Besides*, she told herself, *how many people know who I am anyway?*

Beau greeted her from behind the end of the bar facing the front entry.

"This is quite a turnout," she observed as she stepped up to the counter across from him. She usually avoided tall counters since they only drew attention to her height deficiency, but it felt better to recognize someone in the place.

"It is," he agreed. "How do you like your new iPhone?"

Kevin! "How did you know I got an iPhone?"

He pointed his right thumb over his right shoulder.

She had to take two steps to her left to see around the big man. Kevin stood at the other end of the tavern with a crowd of people gathered around him. Nathan was next to him behind the bar.

"They're getting ready to draw the name," said Beau. "Why don't you go on down there. They were talking about letting you draw the name out of the hat if you showed up."

"No thanks. I think I've got a better view right here." *If they call me down there I'll go.*

"What can I get you, then?"

"How about tonic water?"

"Do you want any gin or vodka in it?"

"No thanks."

"Lime?"

"Absolutely." She placed a five-dollar bill on the bar.

"Hear ye, hear ye," Kevin shouted. He was using a booming voice she had never heard before. "We are gathered here to strike a blow against technology. Not to overthrow it, for we could not live without it. But to periodically re-establish that it is our servant and not the other way around. Occasionally, we, for our own sanity, must assert the dignity of man over the convenience of technology. So before we draw the name, let us hear from you. How has technology degraded you?"

No one spoke for a while.

Beau sat Nattie's drink down just as the uproar started. The first person to respond yelled out, "I hate waiting for a red light to change when I'm in the only car in sight." After that, people yelled things from all over the room, rendering none of them discernible.

"Put your money away," Beau yelled as he leaned across the bar to be heard.

"OK, OK," yelled Nathan with his hands held up over his head. When the room was quiet again, he continued, "I think it's time to draw the name." With that, he bent down behind the bar.

While Nathan was out of sight, Kevin noticed Nattie for the first time and began waving at her to come join him. He pantomimed drawing the name from the hat. It was an act that would put her awkwardly at the center of attention.

Smiling at Beau, she took her drink and left the money.

As she made her way around the outside of the crowd, she heard Nathan's voice again. "Young lady," he said to someone she could not see, "would you be willing to draw the name out of the hat for us?"

Nattie stopped, enveloped by a sudden rush of embarrassment. *It's no one's fault*, she told herself. *Nathan didn't know Kevin signaled me to come down. He couldn't see me, and I told him I wasn't coming.* This all happened so quickly that no one would have noticed unless they were focusing exclusively on her, and no one in the bar was doing that.

The woman he asked to draw the name must have agreed and come forward because the crowd gave her a hand. Then she heard Nathan say, "Randi Lester, ladies and gentleman," a remark that earned another round of applause.

Nattie froze. There would be no recovery from this. She waited until her breathing was back to normal, then quietly made for the door.

CHAPTER 26

POLICE CALL ABOUT ELI

Nattie looked at the clock on the night table next to her bed. The red numbers told her it was 1:30 a.m. Confused about whether or not she had actually been asleep, she was aware that her phone had been ringing. It took another moment before she became aware of what to do.

"Hello," she mumbled.

"Is this Natalie Moreland?"

"Yes."

"This is Officer Early at the Bristol, Tennessee, Police Department."

"John Early?"

"You remember me?"

"I do. You once took care of me after I was knocked unconscious in my parking lot."

"I assume you've fully recovered from that?"

"I have, thank you." She sat up and rubbed her eyes. "Is there something I can do for you, Officer Early?"

"There is. Earlier this evening we picked up a youth on a vandalism charge. It's a bogus charge and we're ready to cut him loose; but he's a minor, and we can't just let him go."

"I don't understand. Where do I fit in?"

"He says he wants to be taken to your house."

"My house?" Nattie was fully awake now.

"Yes. He says he stays there sometimes and his mother gives her permission as long as it is OK with you. So is it?"

"Is it?" she repeated.

"Is it OK with you for us to bring the youth to your house?"

"Is it OK with me?" By this time she was standing up and pacing. "I don't know. Who is it anyway?"

"His name is Eli Anderson."

Thirty minutes later Nattie and Eli were sitting at her kitchen table drinking cranberry juice.

"Tell me, Eli," she finally said. "What were you doing out at one o'clock in the morning?"

"I wasn't doing nothing."

"You weren't doing anything." She corrected him. "If you weren't doing anything, then why did the police waste their time picking you up?"

"They didn't pick me up. That man called them on me."

"But you weren't doing anything?"

Eli's face reddened. "I was cleaning up his garbage. That's what I was doing."

"Calm down, Eli. I was just asking. Besides, if you're going to use my home as a safe house, then I think an explanation is the least you should offer me."

She watched his shoulders drop and stoop forward as if her words had poked a hole in his balloon.

"That sounded like a lecture, didn't it?" she asked.

Eli shrugged his shoulders. "I guess. Maybe it did a little."

"Look, friend, I remember what it felt like to be thirteen and at the mercy of adults who weren't all that adult."

From his deflated slouch Eli stole a glance at her.

"Why don't you just tell me about your evening?"

"What do you want to know?"

"Whatever you want to tell me, Eli. It's your story."

"Mom and I were going to go see the new Harry Potter movie," he started. "She had her keys in her hand and she was reaching for the front door when her phone rang." He stopped talking.

130

After a short wait Nattie asked, "Was it your father?"

Eli stiffened and glared. "I told her not to answer it."

"But she did."

"Nothing," he said, mimicking his mother in a witchy voice. "I know he asked her what she was doing."

Nattie frowned as she watched him.

Eli rolled his eyes and exhaled deeply before continuing. "I just turned around and went to my room."

"Didn't she try to say something? Explain? Anything?"

"She called my name out."

"What did you do?"

"I just shut the door and gave her the finger."

"Did that make you feel better?"

"Yes," he answered curtly.

Sure it did. "Is that when you left?"

"No. I waited until I heard him come in and then I left. They'll never miss me."

"What did you do after you left?"

"I just walked around."

"You weren't going anywhere?"

"No."

"You didn't have any kind of plan?"

"Not really."

"Were you going to end up here again?"

He snuck a peak at her without moving his head.

"Forget I asked that question," she said, waving her hand. "Go on with your story."

"That's it. I was just walking around. I was in front of a real nice house over on Pinehurst, and I saw that this dog had knocked over their garbage can. So I chased the dog away and I was picking stuff up when this fat guy came out and started yelling at me."

"Did you explain what happened?"

"What would be the point?"

"Well, it might have kept you out of the police station."

"I didn't care about that."

Or maybe that would have been the point.

"What did he think, I was stealing, his eggshells?"

131

"Sometimes," explained Nattie, "people go through garbage to steal someone else's identity."

"Who keeps their identity in the garbage?"

Nattie chuckled. "When did the police get there?"

"He had his cell phone and called them with me standing right there."

"What did you do when he was calling the police?"

"I sat down and waited."

"Smart," she noted. "If you had run you might have looked guiltier. What happened when the police got there?"

"They talked to him first and he said he caught me going through his garbage. They asked me what happened and I told them about the dog and what I was doing. I was still holding a half of a grapefruit rind; so when they asked me about that, I told them it was in my hand when the fat guy caught me."

"Did they believe you?"

"They looked around first, but then they asked him if I was holding the grapefruit when he came out and he said I was. Then the cop said it looked to him like my story was accurate because the bag had been torn open like a dog would do it. Then he said there was a bag in the can with papers in it that an identity thief would have torn open instead of picking up grapefruit rinds."

"So the police backed you up. That felt good, didn't it?"

Eli shook his head. "They still asked him if he wanted to press charges."

"They had to do that, Eli. He made the call. But it sounds like they discouraged him from doing so."

"Well, he shouldn't have had a choice because I didn't do nothing."

"I'm sorry, Eli. That's just the way the world is. You tried to help him, and it turned out badly. But you are a Good Samaritan. You did the right thing, and I hope you don't let this keep you from doing the right thing in the future."

A hint of a smile crossed Eli's lips as he finished his cranberry juice.

"Now, can I ask you about something else?"

"Sure."

"Do you know what a double negative is?"

Eli shook his head, no.

"It's when you put two negatives in a sentence."

Eli raised his eyebrows and cocked his head.

"You've used the phrase 'I didn't do nothing' a couple of times."

"Well, I didn't."

"You didn't do anything," she corrected.

"I know."

"But that is not what you said. You said you didn't do nothing."

"Yeah."

"When you use two negatives, they cancel each other out. So if you say you didn't do nothing, it means you did, in fact, do something."

"Of course. You have to do something, don't you?"

"Exactly. You see it is impossible to actually do nothing."

"I agree."

"Good," she sighed.

"If doing nothing is impossible, then no one can do it, right?" he asked.

Scrunching her face, Nattie leaned forward.

"That's all I said," he continued. "No one can do nothing, and I didn't either."

"I'm going to bed," she said, standing up. "There's a blanket and a pillow on the couch in the living room."

CHAPTER 27

NATTIE AND DEBBIE GO TO J.C.

"What are you going to do," asked Debbie, "adopt him?"

She and Nattie had driven to Earth Fare in Johnson City for brown rice cakes and an assortment of other health food items that Debbie's husband, Duane, wanted. On the way there the discussion had mostly centered on books. Both women agreed that *Eat, Love, Pray* was too whiny for them. Neither had finished it. Debbie was nearing the end of *The Help* by Kathryn Stockett and she gave it five stars. The subject of Nattie's late-night visitor had not come up until they were loading their purchases into the back of Debbie's SUV.

I hope not. "Absolutely not," answered Nattie, opening the door to Rita's. They had enjoyed a healthy lunch of salad and Brunswick stew at Earth Fare and were rewarding themselves at what Debbie claimed was the best frozen custard place she had ever been.

Debbie ordered a Misto, "with pina colada custard and sugar-free raspberry Italian ice, please." She explained, "They mix an ice and a custard-like milkshake. It's the most refreshing thing for me."

The mix reminded Nattie too much of a creamsickle, which she found distasteful to the point of revulsion. "Just the peach Italian ice for me," she ordered. It was difficult for her to resist anything sporting the label "Italian."

"So?" Debbie asked, as they settled into one of the picnic tables in front of the store.

"It's delicious," Nattie mumbled with her mouth full. "I've never had anything quite like it."

Debbie dismissed the response with a flip of her hand. "No, I mean so what happened with the kid? Was he there when you got up?"

"Oh, that. No he was already gone, but he left me a tray of lemon poppy seed muffins and a pot of coffee."

"Are you serious? That muffin you brought me this morning was from him?"

Nattie nodded.

"I knew it was homemade. I just thought you made it."

Through a crooked smile, Nattie admitted, "I was kind of hoping you would think that."

Debbie's eyes got bigger. "Maybe you should adopt him."

"Yeah, that's a good idea. And I'll do that just as soon as I can afford to put a liposuction doc on retainer."

Debbie held out a spoon full of her Misto. "When you find one, I'll go halvesies with you."

"It's a deal." After a bit of silence while each enjoyed their treat, Nattie confessed, "I'm worried about him."

"The kid?"

"His name is Eli. He's a nice kid."

"Other than the fact that he keeps breaking into your house when you're asleep."

"There's that, but he means no mischief when he breaks in, and he often leaves my home better than he found it."

"But still, he's a thirteen-year-old boy. What do you think he thinks about while he's sleeping on your couch and you are right upstairs?"

"I think he's thinking how nice it is to be inside instead of wandering around outside."

Debbie rolled her eyes. "Yeah, that's exactly how the mind works in a thirteen-year-old boy. And maybe one day he'll catch a leprechaun, and then he'll share the pot of gold with you."

"OK, give me a break. I know he's probably got some fantasies going in his little head. But if any of them are of me, I don't want to know about it."

Debbie cupped her mouth and in a low voice chanted, "Ostrich."

"I just don't see any benefit in imagining what he's thinking. He's a very nice boy, who needs a lot of help right now. And whether or not I like it, I'm the one in the position to do something about it. What do I do, turn him away? I can't do that. I'm not going to do that. And I'm not going to worry about what he's thinking, either. As long as he treats me with respect, I don't care what is in his imagination."

Debbie leaned toward her and stared.

"What?"

"He may be respectful now," warned Debbie. "He's only thirteen now, and he's frightened and awkward. But you are not taking in to consideration that thirteen-year-old boys become seventeen-year-old boys. And when it comes to sex, seventeen-year-old boys are more likely to overcome their fear and awkwardness."

It was Nattie's turn to lean forward and stare. "What happened to you?"

"Nothing bad, but I had to fight off more than one seventeen-year-old in the backseat of a car."

"OK, then," conceded Nattie, "it's settled. I will not, under any circumstances, get into the backseat of a car with him."

Debbie frowned.

"Unless, of course, he opens his own restaurant on the Amalfi coast of Italy."

"Seriously, Nattie. It may not be a problem now but it could get to be a problem pretty fast."

"I hear you, Deb. I really do."

Nodding to each other signaled that the treat break was over, and it was time to head home.

Walking to the car, Nattie added, "I'll be careful."

Debbie finished buckling herself in and opened her mouth to say something when her phone rang. She looked at the phone number before answering. "Hi, honey," she said into the phone and then mouthed to Nattie that it was Duane. She turned her attention back to the phone. "I'm on my way home from Earth Fare."

Nattie watched her friend.

"No, Nattie's with me."

Hearing her name was a cue for Nattie to turn away.

"I can put her on the phone. Do you want to talk to her?" She looked at Nattie who had turned back to face her. With the phone still against her head she shrugged. Her face had reddened.

"This is silly. I didn't call because I was doing exactly what I told you I would be doing. It took longer because we stopped at Rita's."

Nattie listened to the awkward silence.

"Well, Nattie had never been there before so we stopped."

Nattie had become uncomfortable listening to this conversation, but at this point she had had enough. Digging her earphones out of her bag, she tuned her iPhone into the Loreena McKennitt Pandora station and, through the passenger window, watched the scenery pass by. This is how they rode until Debbie stopped in front of her house.

"I'm sorry about the phone call." Debbie shook her head back and forth quickly. "He gets that way sometimes."

They were standing behind Debbie's SUV. Nattie was collecting the two bags that were hers.

"No problem," Nattie said.

Debbie slammed her back gate shut. "I hate to keep on this, but I think you should do something about the kid."

"OK, then," declared Nattie, "tell me what you would do."

"If it were me, I'd fix that backdoor lock."

"You are really worried for nothing, Deb. He's a nice kid."

"But sometimes," said Debbie as she hugged Nattie good-bye, "the ones that seem nice can turn out to be the most vicious."

CHAPTER 28

NATTIE TALKS TO THE DUKE AGAIN

Detective Schneider was waiting outside the Starbucks at exit seven along Route 81 when Nattie drove into the parking lot. Dressed in a brown checked suit with a pale blue vest and a dark brown hat, he looked every bit as out of place as he had the first time they met at Allison's Restaurant. He raised his hat and opened the door as she approached. "Good morning to you, Miss Moreland," he said, bowing his head in greeting.

"And to you, Detective. Thank you." The fact that he got her name right at their second meeting was not lost on her.

Nattie got her regular coffee immediately and found a table outside where they could speak privately. His decaf coffee had to be brewed separately, requiring that he wait.

"I don't understand why a coffee shop has to make singles of decaffeinated coffee," he said as he joined her out front.

"I know what you mean. I usually have decaf myself, but since this is my first cup of the day, I went ahead and got regular so I wouldn't have to wait."

"But," he noted, placing his hat on the edge of the table, "you had to wait for me."

"On the contrary, I didn't wait. I got us a table."

Glancing around the front walk, he observed, "I see you chose a table out of anyone's earshot."

"You already knew I wanted to talk when I asked to meet you," she pointed out.

"True. How can I be of service?"

"I'm still working the Frank Lester case."

"I figured as much."

They watched each other for a moment before Nattie broke the silence. "I assume you are wondering why I'm not meeting with Detective Quayle."

"It would be a natural thing to do. It is, after all, his case," he said with a gentle smile. "I'm sure you have your reasons and will tell me in good time."

"Thank you for that."

"Not at all."

"Since you are being so gracious with me, can I be direct with you?"

"Certainly. That will be the most expedient approach for each of us."

"Well, here's the bottom line. I don't believe that it is unreasonable for Beau Robinette to be a suspect, but there's not a shred of hard evidence against him."

"No hard evidence yet," he corrected her. "But there is the pattern."

"The presumed pattern." She took her turn to correct.

A quick nod of his head punctuated his response. "Point taken."

"My concern is not that Beau is a suspect," she explained. "I simply think it is odd that no other suspects are being considered."

"Do you know that no other suspects are being considered?"

"I asked Detective Quayle directly for a number of other suspects. I made it clear that I was not looking for any details, just the number. And he got furious with me."

"I see."

"Would you have given me that number if I had asked you?"

"Most certainly."

"Can I be frank?"

He nodded yes.

"It looks to me like Detective Quayle has some sort of grudge against Beau Robinette."

"Are you asking me if I know of a reason for such a grudge?"

"I know it may put you in a bad spot with a fellow officer, but—" She paused. "I didn't know what else to do."

"Not to worry," he said with eyes shut and a slight shake of his head. "There is some history between Hank and your client. You have probably noticed that Hank is—" He looked up as if searching for a word. "Quirky."

"It is hard not to notice."

"My understanding is that he had a brain injury in college, and it changed his personality. But, Miss Moreland, I can assure you that he is a very good detective. His closure rate is very high, even if his social skills are not."

Nattie placed her hand over her heart. "I am not out to get him."

Detective Schneider nodded. "If I thought you were out to get him, we would not be having this conversation. I believe you have a right to understand what you are a party to, and that is why I am answering your question. May I continue?"

"Please do."

"When Officer Robinette was still with Washington County P.D, he noticed Hank's quirkiness and told the higher-ups that he might be dangerous."

Nattie's head recoiled slightly.

"They made Hank go through a grueling series of psychological tests, which he passed with no problems; but it embarrassed him immensely."

"So there is a reason he is solely focusing on Mr. Robinette. Shouldn't he excuse himself from the case if there could be some question about his objectivity?"

"If it is true that no other leads are being pursued, then you are right; he should pass the case off. But you do not know that. What you know is he got angry."

"He got angry because I asked for a number."

"He got angry because an attractive young woman questioned his character."

Nattie flinched to hear herself referred to this way, but the detective continued. "No, the question of other suspects is still to be answered. Rest assured I will get that answer and will inform you in due course."

"I appreciate that, but there is another issue." Nattie leaned forward. "A much bigger issue regarding conflict of interest."

"I assume that you are referring to his history with Frank Lester?"

"You know about that?"

"Of course. You look surprised."

"To tell you the truth, I am surprised. Why would he be allowed to continue?"

"This isn't a big city. We often have to investigate cases in which we know someone. We take pains to avoid that when doing so might interfere with an investigation or give a defense attorney an edge. In this case, neither seems likely."

"Why do you say that?"

"Because when the case first came through, Hank asked for it and disclosed his history with the victim. You see Hank Quayle is a deeply religious man and he asked for the case as a way to bring forgiveness and then closure to his relationship with Mr. Lester."

"Are you serious?"

"Absolutely. When Hank finds whoever is guilty, his history with the victim will not jeopardize his case. If anything, he could be accused of being sympathetic toward the guilty."

"That's the point. Hank himself has a motive. He could be guilty."

"Oh my."

"Oh my? Surely someone has thought of that."

"Surely someone has. But I must admit it is not something I considered until you just mentioned it." Schneider grimaced before continuing. "I fear this is a bit embarrassing to my status as a detective. It says something about my attitude toward his character and my trust in our supervisors doing their job. Still, as a detective I should have at least considered the possibility."

"Please, Detective, don't be embarrassed. We are all human," Nattie told him in a soft voice.

"Thank you. Can I ask a favor of you?"

"What?"

"Please call me Duke."

"OK—Duke."

"Thank you. And now I must run. I will find out if other suspects are being considered and I will find out what sort of alibi Hank has."

"And you will let me know?"

He nodded. "And what is next for your investigation?"

"I'm still searching through Lester's history looking for someone with a motive."

CHAPTER 29

NATTIE INTERVIEWS ROD THRIFT

Jefferson International University sat in a picturesque valley among the rolling hills of southwest Virginia about an hour north and east of Abingdon. It was a little past eleven when Nattie walked into the building looking for Rod Thrift's name on the marquee. She found the name "Viceroy Thrift" listing an office on the second floor.

Viceroy Thrift's office was the first office on the hallway facing the stairway. The door was closed. She knew she was in the right place because the first half of the nameplate on the door was covered with a piece of white trainer's tape with the name "Rod" written on it with a red marker. There was also a yellow Post-it Note on the door that read, "Come in if you have donuts; otherwise, go away."

Nattie hesitated in front of the door until she heard someone call out to her from down the hallway, "Are you Natalie Moreland?"

She turned to watch a tall man with a big belly and spindly legs approaching her. "Yes. Are you Coach Thrift?"

"I am indeed." He got close enough to see that she had noticed his sign. "Oh don't worry about that. It's just my way of saying 'I'm not in right now; but if you have donuts, come on in.' I'm sorry if it threw you off." Patting his middle, "Most everybody who knows me knows what that means. Come on in."

"I didn't bring any donuts," she informed him.

"Oh don't worry about that," he repeated, opening the door. As she walked by, he added, "You can owe me."

He took a stack of folders off one of the chairs across from his desk. Assuming that chair was intended for her she sat down.

"You are here to talk about Frankie Lester, right?"

She nodded.

"What did he do?"

"I'm sorry?"

"What did Frankie do to bring you to see his old college baseball coach?"

The question certainly meant that he had no delusions about Frank Lester. "He got himself attacked," she answered curtly, hoping to catch him off guard.

"One of his fans no doubt. Was he hurt badly?"

"A couple of broken ribs, a broken thigh bone that has him in traction, and a bump on the head that gave him a nasty headache for a few days."

Rod Thrift shrugged indifferently.

"There is no credible suspect at the moment, so I'm checking into anyone from his past that might still be holding a grudge against him."

Rod Thrift put his hands on the edge of his desk and, pushing himself backward, laughed heartily, "I might as well send you the entire roster from his freshman and sophomore years. He was gone after that." After getting more composed, he amended his suggestion, "Actually, he was OK in his freshman year. At least he was OK with his teammates. When he came to us he was as fiery a competitor as I have ever seen. He backed down from nothing, from no one. If one of his teammates got into it with someone, he was the first one off the bench. I finally told the bullpen coach to sit on him. He was our closer. That's something for a freshman. Do you know what a closer is?"

"The relief pitcher is the one who comes in to pitch the last inning if your team is winning."

144

Coach Thrift was obviously impressed. "Yes, that's right. But with Frankie I could bring him in to pitch the last two or three innings. He was really something. Arm of steel, I'll tell you. I could have pitched him every day. We thought we really had something going into his sophomore year. We told him he'd be a starter the next year. We already had a righty with a ninety–two-mile-an-hour fastball and another lefty who threw junk. Frankie had a curve ball that looked like it dropped off a table. Do you know how many teams there are at our league with two legitimate professional prospects in their rotation? I'll tell you, not many, and we had three."

Nattie had been nodding in a way to tell him she was following his story and did not need a lesson in baseball; however, seeing it was to no avail, she decided to nudge him along. "What happened in his sophomore year?"

"He changed. It became his team. He'd go after teammates if he thought they weren't hustling enough. I don't mean get on them. Coaches like players like that. No, he'd browbeat them in public. You know, make a big scene and embarrass them."

"I'm surprised that didn't get him into a few fights."

"Every— single—" The coach gritted his teeth trying to find a substitute word for the one he was thinking. "It happened nearly every day. It was a nightmare."

"I'm surprised the school didn't get involved."

"We were able to contain it, at least for a while. We should have seen it coming, though."

"Why is that?"

"Like I said, we thought he was just a hot-headed freshman and that he'd mellow out as he got older. That's the way it usually works, but not him. At the banquet at the end of the season we gave him the 'Freshman of the Year' award; and when he accepted, he stuck his fist out to show everyone the tattoo he had put on his right hand."

"The four aces on the upper part of each finger," she offered.

"You've seen it, then?"

"I saw him in the hospital once."

"He hasn't changed much, has he?"

"Not as far as I can tell."

"That figures," Thrift said, shaking his head. Then he exhaled and continued his story. "He put the tattoo on himself, designating himself as the ace of our staff. Now that is some set of—" Again he searched for words. "He basically told two seniors he was coming for them."

"How did that go over?"

"The lefty junk-ball pitcher laughed it off. I think he really thought it was funny. He was slotted in the number two slot anyway."

"The righty with the fastball was the ace, then?"

"He had been the ace all year and was going to be the next year, as well. Now he—his name is Trace—Trace took it personal. It probably was personal too."

"How do you mean?"

"For one thing, the tattoo was Trace's idea. Frank put four aces across the knuckles on his pitching arm; but long before that, Trace had the letters F I R E tattooed across the knuckles on his pitching arm. So you see, the gesture was aimed at Trace specifically. Old Frankie's fastball was never in the nineties, but he always hit whatever he was aiming at."

"You said 'for one thing.' Is there something else?"

"Oh yeah. The two of them had been at each other all spring. You see, Trace had this girlfriend. A real looker," Thrift added, then, realizing what he had said, blushed. "I think they had dated for a while. She came to all our games and most of our practices the year before Frankie got there."

"Then she and Frank Lester started up together," guessed Nattie.

"That's right." The coach pointed a thumb at her. "I mean no offense, young lady, but sometimes women can really be trouble for young men."

"No offense taken," said Nattie. "I'm sure Frank Lester was destined to be a model citizen if it hadn't been for that 'real looker' woman."

Coach Thrift looked directly at her for a moment. Nattie wondered if he was going to get angry, but then his face broke out in a grin. "I deserved that, didn't I?"

"Yes," she said, "but you took it well."

He laughed again.

"So what happened the next year, Coach?"

"Neither Carmine nor Trace played fall ball that next year. Carmine— that's the other lefty—had some kind of internship he was doing in

146

Baltimore. It was for med school or something. And Trace was ineligible because of grades."

"So Frankie turned out to be the ace, then."

"True, at least for half the fall season. Then he got himself permanently banned from the NCAA and quit school." Sitting back and resting his hands behind his head, he said, "That's the last time I ever saw him, and I am fine with that. Does any of that help you?"

"Maybe," she answered. "At least it confirms what I have already come to believe about him. Who knows, maybe one of his former teammates will know something. I'd like to take you up on that offer to have the team roster from his sophomore year."

"I can't give you one. That is, I don't think I could actually find one for you in this mess; but it's on the team Web site if you know how to do that kind of thing."

"Of course. Thanks. What's Trace's last name, if you don't mind?"

"Noble."

She wrote Trace Noble's name down in her Moleskine. "Can you think of another teammate that you think I should especially seek out?"

"If I had to pick the most likely candidate it would hands down be Trace Noble, but Trace was a little like Frankie."

"How do you mean?"

"Well, either of them could find a reason to hold a grudge easier than a monkey could find his own—" He paused without finishing his sentence. "Either of them could form a grudge, but I doubt either of them could wait this long to get even."

You probably got that right about Frankie, anyway. "How about the girl, Trace's girlfriend? Do you remember her name?"

"I don't know her last name, but her first name was Randi."

CHAPTER 30

RANDI REMEMBERS

"I'm sorry if I was short with you last night when I answered the phone."

"I didn't think you were short, Randi," answered Nattie. "It just sounded like I caught you at a bad time."

Randi looked down without responding.

The momentary self-righteous delight she felt in knowing the married woman "involved" with her ex-husband was hurting was immediately replaced by guilt for having such a reaction. "I'm sorry," Nattie said. "I should have waited until today to call you."

Looking back up, Randi asked, "How could you have known I was having a rough night?"

The question surprised Nattie, partly because it exposed her tendency to be overly responsible, but mostly because it was insightful. As fair-minded as Nattie liked to consider herself, she still held the belief that women who looked like Randi were not supposed to be insightful. "No, you're right. I couldn't have known. But I am sorry that it upset you."

"Thank you for that, but it actually was good for me to come out of the cave I was in. I had a therapy session that evening and it really tore me up."

"Do you want to talk about it?"

"That's nice of you to offer."

Especially when you're still hanging around Nathan. "No, really."

She studied Nattie's face. "I think you mean that."

"I do."

Her eyes reddened, "I don't think I'm ready to talk about it more, but it's nice that you offered."

"Really, Randi, I mean it. I'm not a counselor, but I am a good listener and I'm here right now if you want."

"OK," Randi said meekly, scooting forward. "I think I can tell you without falling apart again. My therapist wanted me to find some women to confide in." She contorted her face for a moment, the way a child might do when she was about to say something childish. "I suppose you are the closest thing I have to a woman friend."

Nattie smiled, but inside she was flinching. She did not want to become Randi's only female confidante.

"My mother died in a car accident when I was twelve years old."

"I remember you telling me that."

"Did I also tell you that my brother was driving the car she was in?"

"You did."

"Well, he was sixteen and still driving on his permit so my mother had to go with him. She was waiting in the car for him and I had just come back in through the front door when he put his hand up my blouse. Did I tell you all that too?"

"You did."

"Well," said Randi, "I'm sure I also told you what I yelled at him."

"'I hope you die,'" answered Nattie gently. "You did tell me that too."

"OK, then, I told you everything I had remembered up to that point. But more has come back. After I said that to my brother, my mother rolled the window down and said, 'we'll deal with it when we get home.' But we weren't going to deal with it. We never dealt with it. So I stood there while he backed out of the driveway and waited for them to look at me. Then," she swallowed and tipped her head forward, "then I screamed, 'I hope you both die.'" She exhaled loudly and slumped forward.

Nattie held her silence and watched Randi's shoulders rise and fall with her breathing.

It took a good bit of time for Randi to look back up. When she did, her eyes were red but she had not cried. "Wow," she sighed, "I'm surprised I could do that. I guess I cried it all out last night."

"I'm not really sure what to say," confessed Nattie.

"There isn't anything to say. I know I didn't kill my mother. I just didn't know I was holding on to that memory."

"You can know something and still believe something else," observed Nattie.

"I found that out." Then reaching across the table, Randi placed her hand on top of Nattie's and gently squeezed. Her touch was tender and warm. Then with a start she blushed and abruptly let go.

"So," she said, regaining her composure, "did you want to talk about something to do with your investigation?"

"I do. I know I asked you once if you knew anyone who might have a grudge against Frank; and you said it could be anyone, but that no one especially stood out. Is that still true?"

"Yes. I would have called you immediately if I had thought of something else, but I haven't."

"I'm sure that's true, Randi. I'm not doubting your sincerity. It's just that I have started looking further back in his history and wonder if maybe you had any ideas about someone from his college days who might still be holding a grudge."

"Oh sure. Probably half the people he played baseball with." Her eyes got big. "In fact, do you know that detective who's working on the case?"

"Henry Quayle?"

"Yeah, him. Frank beaned him once."

"Really?" Nattie said, acting surprised.

"Really. It was bad too. I was there. I thought Frank killed him." Randi shook her head slowly. "That's what cost him his career."

"Why is that?"

"After that, he was kicked out of school. He couldn't pitch in college anymore, and then no pro scout would talk to him."

"Would you say Detective Quayle might be a candidate for beating Frank up? I mean, he certainly has motive."

"No, I don't think so. I don't think he has the strength to do the kind of damage that was done to Frank. Do you?"

"I don't know," answered Nattie. "Can you think of anyone else?"

150

"Well there was this guy that I dated right before I started going out with Frank."

Here it comes, thought Nattie.

"He wasn't an athlete. He was a photography major, the best in our class."

What about Trace Noble? "Were you photography major?"

"I was," she answered tentatively. "But that was a long time ago."

"Do you still do it?"

"Do I still take pictures?"

Nattie nodded.

"Sometimes, not often, though."

"Well if you loved it once, maybe it would be good to take it up again."

"Charlotte says that too."

"So, Randi, where is this photographer now? Could he be the one who attacked Frank?"

"Oh, I doubt that. He's in Paris now photographing fashion models. I can't imagine he even remembers me."

"Well, think about it. Is there anyone else from college that might still act on a grudge against Frank? Maybe someone else you dated?" Nattie wondered, *Is she noticing that I'm pressing?*

Randi looked quizzically at Nattie. "Do you mean Trace?"

She noticed. "I do. I was up at Jefferson yesterday and talked to the baseball coach. He told me there was some bad blood between those two men."

"That's true."

"According to coach Thrift, Frank took you away from Trace."

"No. There was bad blood between them, but it had nothing to do with me. Trace broke it off with me over that summer. I was on an art history tour in Europe that summer."

"With the photographer?"

"Yes."

"What happened with him?"

"To tell you the truth, I don't know. He was the nicest guy I ever dated. He was kind, funny, gentle, and thoughtful. He was just about perfect except for one thing." She held up a single finger. "He bored me silly."

"So you broke it off with him?"

"As soon as we got back, I ended it."

"So what happened between him and Frank?"

"He had some pictures of me from the Europe trip, and he put them in a book and brought them to me at a baseball game because he knew I'd be there. It was just a sweet thing to do. He wasn't trying anything, but Frank went nuts and tore it up in front of him. Dalton could not believe it. He stood there with his mouth open, and then he said, 'I feel sorry for you.' Frank laughed at him." She turned away before continuing. "I can still see the look on his face. It was pity. I could picture him thinking, 'You must be out of you mind to pick this caveman over me.' I don't know if he really thought that or not, but he should have. I know I have."

Nattie held her tongue again.

"The bad blood between Frank and Trace is probably because they are exactly the same. They both think they can have whatever they want, and they just take whatever they want. Neither one of them ever said they were sorry for anything. Nothing was ever their fault. And I went from one to the other, like that's what I was looking for."

"That would be good to talk to Charlotte about."

Randi nodded emphatically. "Oh, it's come up a time or two."

"So, do you think Trace could be our attacker?"

"No, he's like Frank. Neither of them could hold a grudge that long without acting on it. Their pride, you know. But now that you make me think about it again, there was something odd that happened about a year ago."

"What?" asked Nattie excitedly.

"Frank was in Afghanistan, and I noticed he got a call from Trace on his phone bill. I asked Frank about it, and he said he didn't know what it was about. He told me to send the bill to him, and he'd check it out. So I did. I didn't think about it again until I noticed that his bills stopped coming home."

"How did he explain that?"

She frowned as she recalled his words, "He told me I was crazy."

152

CHAPTER 31

NATTIE INTERVIEWS TRACE

Trace Noble's office was on the second floor of a three-story building on Broad Street in downtown Kingsport. The diagonal parking in the center of the street made it easy for her to spot the bright yellow Thunderbird with the "FIRE" vanity plates. Boys and their toys, she chided. You sure don't make yourself hard to find.

The sign on the glass door read "Youngblood Enterprises." The first thing Nattie noticed as she entered was how cold it was. The second thing she noticed was the thick sweater the older woman at the copier was wearing.

"You must be Ms. Moreland," the receptionist said. "I'll tell Mr. Noble that you are here. Would you like some coffee? I have hot water for tea. Or would you rather have bottled water?"

"I'm fine, thank you."

With her hand on the door at the back of the office, the woman added, "Well, you just let me know if you change your mind."

"Thank you," Nattie said, but the woman had already opened the door and her head had disappeared into the room beyond. After a moment, the head reappeared and the door swung open. Trace Noble made his entrance. He was well dressed in dark suit pants, suspenders, and starched white shirt rolled up at the sleeves and a silk tie. His fashion sense was somewhere between a game-show host and a politician to Nattie's reckoning. He looked like Treat Williams.

Showing both rows of teeth with his smile, Trace pointed at her, "You look like that blonde. Oh what is her name? She's made a few movies." He looked at the woman in the thick sweater. "Come on Madge, help me out here."

"Jennifer Aniston," guessed Madge; but when she noticed the reaction she got, she added, "I don't know. Who do people say you look like?"

"I get told I look like Kristen Bell sometimes," answered Nattie reluctantly.

"Yes, that's it, Kristen Bell." Extending his hand as he marched across the room Trace introduced himself, adding, "I get the Treat Williams question a lot."

"Nattie Moreland." As she took his hand, Nattie observed that his grip was solid, but made no sign of trying to "prove" anything.

"You met Madge?"

"Yes, of course."

"Did she tell you about her pet pig?"

Madge blushed. "She doesn't want to hear about that."

"She has a pet pig."

"It's a pot-bellied pig," explained Madge. "It's an inside pet."

Cupping his mouth with one hand and lowering his voice, Trace whispered, "It uses kitty litter." He turned to Madge. "Tell Ms. Moreland what the pig's name is, Madge."

Madge waited until she had Nattie's full attention, "Hambone."

Trace snickered. "The pig's name is Hambone. Isn't that great?"

Madge waited for Trace's laughter to subside. "He's the one who came up with that name."

Is this a show? wondered Nattie as she watched the playful interchange. So far she had seen nothing in Trace Noble that seemed remotely similar to Frank Lester.

"Come on in," he said to Nattie as Marge handed him several sheets of paper from the copier. "Thanks, Madge." He stood looking over the pages before closing the door.

154

Trace's office was twice the size of the front office, with a bank of windows along the front overlooking Broad Street. To the right was a small round coffee table with five cushy leather chairs set around it. To the left was a large desk with a high-backed leather desk chair where his suit coat draped. The books and artifacts on the bookshelves behind the desk looked like they had not been disturbed since the interior decorator placed them there. The top of the desk, however, looked used, with a coffee cup stain on the right-hand corner, a computer on the left corner, and three stacks of files lined up across the front.

Nattie walked slowly through the office and stood looking out the windows until Trace said, "Nice view, don't you think?"

"It is. It is an impressive office."

He laughed. "It better be. It cost a fortune." Then pointing at the bookcase he admitted, "I don't have any idea what's on those shelves, but image is everything when you're in my line of work."

"What is it that you do exactly, Mr. Noble?"

He gestured for her to sit on one of the leather chairs. "I negotiate deals. We—that means me—own rental properties in Gatlinburg, Blowing Rock, and almost thirty condos along the Florida coast. I have a couple of storage facilities in the Tri Cities and partial ownership of small businesses across Tennessee and Kentucky. I'm always looking for more opportunities."

As Nattie sat in the chair facing the desk with the wall to her back, Trace took the one opposite her. "So, Ms Moreland—can I call you Nattie?"

"Please do."

"So, Nattie, what can I do for you? You said you wanted to talk about the Jefferson baseball team."

"That's right. I believe you were on the team that placed third in the National tournament."

"That's right. Boy, that was a great team. We should have won." Trace shook his head. "You know, with baseball so much depends on who is hot and who is cold. We had a third baseman that was hitting a ton until we reached the semi-finals, and then he went cold. If he had just had an average game, we'd have won easy."

"Still, placing third at the Nationals is quite an accomplishment."

"I know—but we were so close."

"My understanding is that you pitched. Is that right?"

"I had a ninety-four-mile-an-hour fastball." He held out his fist to show Nattie the "FIRE" tattoo across his knuckles. "That's a constant reminder of those days." Retracting his hand and looking at it himself, he lamented, "Ah. The foolishness of youth."

"Do you remember another pitcher on that team named Frank Lester?"

"Lester wasn't on that team. He was the year before, but got himself thrown out in the fall season. What a nut job he was. Yeah, I remember him. How could you forget a guy like him? Why? Is that what this is about?"

"When was the last time you had any contact with Mr. Lester?"

Trace grinned. "What did he do this time? Is he in trouble?"

It was obvious that the adult Trace Noble was not the person described to her by the people who knew him as an adolescent. Nattie decided that direct was the best approach, "On Monday, May the ninth, Frank Lester was attacked with a baseball bat."

"Is he dead?"

"He sustained several severe injuries, including a concussion and a broken thigh bone."

"Wow," said Trace, raising an eyebrow.

"Do you have any idea who might want to hurt him that badly?"

"Do you think it might have been someone from that team?"

"Do you?" asked Nattie.

"That was a long time ago." Trace waved his hand. "No, it couldn't be someone from that team after all this time. Besides, he's probably made hundreds of enemies since then."

"I'd say you are right, Mr. Noble."

"Trace, please."

"Well, Trace, your information is consistent with what we have heard elsewhere so I won't bother you anymore."

"This has been no bother at all. I'm sorry I couldn't have been of more help."

"Now that you mention it, there is one more thing I need from you."

"What is it?"

"This is just a formality, I assure you, but could you tell me where you were and what you were doing on May ninth?"

156

After a brief hesitation, he said, "Sure," and went over to his desk. After typing for a moment he asked, "What was that date again?"

"May ninth."

Nattie watched his face more up and down and left and right until he nodded at the screen and stood back up. "I was in the hospital having an exploratory procedure done on my heart."

"Thank you for checking," she said as she stood and lifted her shoulder bag.

"Is there anything else I can do for you?"

"If it's no trouble, I'd appreciate some sort of documentation about that hospital stay. Anything will do, a bill or a discharge plan or an admissions form, anything that will close this part of the investigation."

"Can you give me a few days to dig that up?"

"Oh sure, and if you can't find anything I'm sure you can have the hospital send me something." She handed him a business card.

"Natasha McMorales," he read out loud.

CHAPTER 32

THE GRAPEFRUIT

"What's that?" asked Kevin, peering over her shoulder.

She held the frame up so he could see.

"Is that the poem the Wolf read at your wedding rehearsal?" Then, taking it from her, he exclaimed, "It is! I thought you lost this."

"Nathan found it. He gave it to me last week."

Kevin handed it back to her before circling the table to sit across from her, "When did you and Nathan get together, sis?"

Ignoring his question, she asked one of her own, "What are you doing here, Kevin? I thought you always had those giant breakfast hamburgers at the Sunny Side Up on Monday mornings."

"I tried, but they weren't open. I don't know what happened."

"It was probably that location with no parking and almost no through traffic. That's what happened." She noticed Kevin staring at her with no indication that he was listening. "What?" she asked.

"You didn't answer my question."

"I did. I told you he gave it to me last week."

He continued to stare.

"What is it, Kevin?"

"You know very well I want to hear more than that. Come on, give me details."

"It was a nice gesture, OK? He found it tucked in the pages of an art book and he had it framed and gave it to me. End of story."

"Right," Kevin said with a sarcastic drawl. "I'm going to get a breakfast bagel. Do you want anything?"

Shaking her head, Nattie pointed at the untouched breakfast wrap sitting on the table in front of her.

"Aren't you going to eat that?"

"Have it," she said pushing the plate to his side of the table.

By the time he returned with his own coffee, she had put the poem away in her shoulder bag.

"So what Nathan did was no big deal, right?" he said, shoving one end of the breakfast wrap into his mouth.

"Drink your coffee, Kevin."

Taking a large gulp, he forced what was in his mouth down his throat. "Mocha Mint. Have you tried it?"

"No, I always get the decaf."

"Of course, why would you ever want to change your mind about something?"

"Nice haircut," she said.

He smiled. "Would you believe he spent an hour up at Carl B. Jesse's Frame Shop picking out the frame? And do you think it was a mere accident where he gave it to you?"

"You knew he gave it to me and you knew where he gave it to me, you—" She could not think of what to call him.

"Cupid?" he suggested with the same grin he had been using since he was three and someone told him he was cute.

"That's not the word I was searching for."

"Well, what were you searching for at Our House the other night?"

"I came to see the death of my BlackBerry. It was mine, wasn't it?"

"Sure. I was glad to see you."

Don't go there, Kevin.

"Why didn't you stay?"

"I got a phone call."

Looking down at his watch, he speculated, "That was just after eight o'clock, I think." After tapping his watch, he added, "I wonder if your phone log will show a call about that time. You wouldn't want to place a little wager on that would you?"

"I can think of the word I want to use now."

Kevin laughed. "I suppose that means no bet."

Staring out the front window allowed her to distance herself from his laugh. "It was just a shock. He told me he wasn't seeing her anymore."

"So you got pissed off?"

"I wasn't pissed off." I was embarrassed. "I was just surprised is all."

"She was there. So what? Does that mean he isn't waiting for you?"

"It's complicated, Kevin."

"It may be complicated, sis, but Randi Lester is not the complication."

"I suppose I'm the complication."

He lifted his coffee cup in salute. "There you go. You get it now."

Nattie reached across the table to retrieve the half of her breakfast wrap he had not yet snarfed. "I'll just go ahead and get this too, if you don't mind." She took a bite. Before she swallowed, she asked, "Tell me about my BlackBerry. Is it dead?"

"I'll show you," he bragged. He took his computer from his backpack on the adjacent chair. "I put this on You Tube. It's called 'Black Friday for BlackBerry.'"

Nattie watched his computer screen as the video opened. The scene was the one she had witnessed herself, with Kevin at the end of the bar speaking into the camera and the people cheering and yelling out their own grievances against technology. Then Nathan's face came into view. He stood on his toes and craned his neck looking for someone in the crowd. The search lasted less than a minute before his shoulders slumped and he beckoned Randi forward to draw the name from the hat. The name that was drawn belonged to a wisp of a girl who did not look like she had the weight to break wind much less a BlackBerry. Next, Kevin set the scene with the designated destroyer wearing a black glove standing at the end of the bar where he had been. Carmina Burana played in the background while he read the "official" grievances against this BlackBerry. When he had finished, the music was turned up loud and the camera zoomed in on the BlackBerry spanning two blocks of wood like a karate board. As soon as the music ended, a giant black-gloved hand, clearly not the hand of the woman wearing the other black glove, came down on the defenseless machine. Kevin's face then appeared close to

160

the camera displaying the BlackBerry's shattered screen and its new V-shaped contour. "This is one Smartphone that won't outsmart anyone again."

"Very clever, Kevin. I especially like the choice of creepy music."

Smiling with pride, he spun the computer around to face himself. "I want to see if I got any comments."

While he played with his computer, Nattie replayed the video in her head. *Was Nathan looking for me?*

Before she could answer her question, Kevin noted, "That's strange." He turned the computer screen toward her. "Look at this."

He came to stand behind her as she tried to decipher what was on the screen. It was an e-mail from Trace Noble. The caption above the picture read, "Here's the results of my heart procedure. Have you ever seen a cleaner looking valve?" Across the picture was an insert with the May ninth date on it. The picture looked like a heart valve.

"What's so strange?" she asked.

He looked at her like she was stupid. "Are you serious?"

"What is it, Kevin?" She could not tell if her mounting frustration was aimed at herself for not getting it or at Kevin for not saying it.

"The picture." He pointed at it and declared, "It's not a heart valve."

Nattie strained her eyes for a closer view of the screen. "What is it then?"

"That is a close-up picture of the center of a grapefruit."

CHAPTER 33

DUKE TAKES NATTIE TO THE NURSING HOME

Where are you taking me? Nattie wondered as she followed Duke Schneider's midnight blue Grand Marquis up Route 81. He had said it would just be a twenty-minute drive, but they were passing exit 19, the last Abingdon exit. They got off Route 81 at an exit she had never noticed before. Two miles later they drove into the parking lot of Del Bella Rosa, an assisted living facility that Nattie had never noticed before either.

"How long has this place been here?" Nattie asked as she exited her Subaru Forester.

"At least twenty years," answered Duke. "Maybe more. It's just two miles off Route 81, but you'd never know it was here from the highway."

As they walked toward the front entrance, he reached into the side pocket of his jacket and took out two plastic cards attached to what looked like long shoelaces. Handing her one, he explained, "These are name badges, or more like passes. We'll need these to get past the front desk."

162

Nattie draped the shoelace around her neck. "And this is going to help with the Frank Lester case, right?"

"Patience," he said with a smile that tested her patience. "This will answer all the questions and concerns about Henry Quayle."

Duke led her through the lobby, by the front desk where the bored young woman barely acknowledged their passes, and down the left hallway of the L-shaped building. Nattie looked at her watch as they passed the dining hall. It was 8:15 in the evening and the room was deserted already.

Duke stood by the last doorway on the right, waiting for her to catch up before entering the large community room.

"B-12," was called out through a sound system.

Vitamins, was Nattie's first thought, but realized quickly that it was a Bingo game. No one seemed to notice them as they stood in the back surveying the room. About forty-five people, thirty of whom were women, were spread out at various tables scattered around the room.

"N-36." The caller stood at a table along the left side of the room rather than the front. He leaned over to choose another number. The banjo around his neck looked oddly out of place. He raised his head to speak into the microphone. "N-41."

It was Henry Quayle. Nattie looked at Duke Schneider, who nodded and said, "He's here every Monday night from seven thirty to nine thirty."

"That's his alibi, then," stated Nattie. As long as it can be verified.

"You'll have to check that out for yourself, of course; but I've been told that he has not missed a Monday night in two years."

"Paul has Bingo!" yelled a woman from the middle of the room.

"Is that right, Paul?" asked Henry through the microphone.

Paul lifted his Bingo card to answer and launched his dried beans into the air causing a good-natured laugh from his tablemates.

"'Moonlight in Vermont,'" yelled Paul.

"Bring me your card first," returned Henry.

Paul handed his card to the woman across from him who took it to the table in front of Henry. Henry's lips moved as he checked to make sure Paul had won. "Ok, Paul," he finally said. "'Moonlight in Vermont' it is."

It took a minute for him to find the music in the satchel on one end of the table. After several drinks from his water bottle and adjustments of his finger picks, Henry began to play the banjo. Nattie wondered if anything could sound worse and then he began singing as well.

"Are you speechless?" asked Duke quietly.

"I'm not sure what to say. That song on a banjo would be quite a trick for a very good banjo player, for him it's— it's—"

"An alibi?" he suggested as the word she was looking for.

At 8:30 Henry announced he would be taking a break. He had just sung "I Want to Hold Your Hand" to resounding applause. Tucking a brown envelope under his arm, he grabbed his water bottle and walked over to join Duke and Nattie where they were waiting.

"Miss Moreland."

"Detective," she answered. "You are quite the entertainer."

Henry offered her a tentative smile. "Thank you for taking care of my travel mug at Zazzy'z last week."

After Duke excused himself, Henry said, "Look, I know you're just doing your job. I was out of line getting mad. I did disclose my history with Frank Lester, but not to you; so how could you have known?"

Nattie nodded.

"And I'm sure when you check it out, you'll find that I was here doing my thing on the banjo on that Monday night."

"I'm sure I will," she agreed. But I will check it out.

"As far as my issues with Beau Robinette go, I think this will speak for itself." He handed her the brown envelope. "I think you'll find this very interesting."

"OK."

"Now I have to go finish out the night. Do you have any requests?"

"Can you play the William Tell Overture?"

He grinned. "I never have, but I don't usually let that get in my way."

Duke got a call and had to leave, which allowed Nattie to slip out unnoticed. She wandered to the third-floor nurses' station.

"Excuse me," Nattie said to the woman behind the desk.

The nurse, a stout woman of about forty-five, nearly jumped a foot off her chair. "Lord love a duck!" she exclaimed, holding both hands on her chest. The book she had been reading sprang shut when she removed her hands.

164

"I'm sorry. I didn't mean to startle you."

"That's not your fault. It's just I thought I was alone. I usually hear them coming." She looked at her watch and then down the hallway. "Folks should be coming back upstairs any time now."

"From Bingo?"

Sitting back down, the woman slid the book into a drawer and ran her finger across a page on a clipboard. "This is Monday isn't it?" she asked.

"It is."

"Then it's Bingo night all right. Is there anything else I can I help you with?"

"As a matter of fact, I'd like a little more information on Bingo night."

"What would you like to know?"

"I want to know about the banjo player."

"I'm not sure what kind of help I can be. I'm always here on the floor on Monday nights, but the members like him a lot. They think he's funny."

"I've been told he has not missed a Monday night in a long time. Could you tell me how long?"

Two voices came from behind Nattie. "Good evening, Millie."

"Good evening, Ruth. Good evening, Ms. Davenport. You are the first ones back." Millie smiled warmly at the two women. "Maybe you can answer this lady's question?"

The two elderly women, standing arm in arm, glanced at each other silently before answering in unison, "Certainly."

Then turning simultaneously to face Nattie, Ruth spoke for both, "What's your question, dear?"

"I've been told the banjo player has not missed a Monday night in a long time. How long would you say it has been?"

"Two or three years," answered Ruth.

"Two and a half years," added Ms. Davenport.

Millie turned to her left. "Good evening, John. Good evening, Thomas."

"Millie," said John, tipping his head.

Ignoring Millie's greeting, Thomas stopped next to Ruth and Ms. Davenport. "What are you two blabbering about? That putz who plays the banjo?"

165

"Wait a minute, Thomas. Where do you get off calling the banjo player a putz?"

"I don't know, John. Where do you get off calling that putz a banjo player?"

CHAPTER 34

NATTIE RETURNS TO JOHNSTON MEMORIAL

Nattie has no idea of what she was hoping to gain out of another visit to Frank Lester's hospital room, but she was fresh out of plans and it was conveniently on the way home. Having nothing to lose but her temper, she decided to stop. When all else fails, shake some trees and see what drops out, she told herself and then immediately wondered what literary detective she was quoting.

She had to hurry to get past the front desk before 10:00 p.m., when visiting hours were over. Once in Frank's room, she knew that her chances of being evicted were slim: nurses rarely enforced the curfew for visitors who were already on the hall. She would have made it too if she had not seen a bright yellow Thunderbird convertible parked on the street below the entrance. After finding a spot in the parking garage she walked back down the hill just to see the license plate. It read "FIRE," confirming her suspicion. Trace Noble was here.

The discovery cost her admission to the hospital, so she made herself as comfortable as she could on the bench in the lobby and began rehearsing the conversation she anticipated with Trace Noble when he came through.

As she settled down, two nurses exited the café. Nattie recognized one of them from Frank Lester's unit the first time she had visited the hospital. They were discussing the transition to the new hospital building.

Nattie interrupted them. "Excuse me."

"Yes."

"I couldn't help hearing you talk about the move to the new building and I was curious about how you moved patients."

"It's not a problem for me," said the nurse Nattie did not recognize. "I work with babies. If we have any to move when the time comes, we can let the moms and babies ride in the ambulette." She pointed at her companion with her thumb. "She's got the tougher unit to transfer."

Nattie looked for a sign of recognition in the other nurse; but seeing none, she said, "I assume some conditions will be harder to move than others."

"Of course," said the nurse she recognized.

"And some patients will be harder to move than others," offered the other. The two nurses exchanged knowing glances.

There was no way for Nattie to know if they were speaking of Frank Lester, but clearly they both knew to which patient the comment was referring.

"Some of my patients are in traction, so the transition is not just about loading all the equipment they need. Even the drive over there has to be done slowly and with great care."

Nattie joked, "So you avoid driving on back roads with those patients."

The nurse from Frank's unit glared at Nattie, but her friend leaned toward her and whispered out of the corner of her mouth, "There's one we'll take through the quarry."

That's got to be Frank, thought Nattie as she watched the two women continue walking.

Twenty minutes later Trace came strolling through the lobby on his way to the front door. The cell phone in his left hand occupied all of his attention and thus afforded her the element of surprise.

"I didn't expect to see you here," she said when he got close enough to touch.

She was sure he had not seen her, but neither did he show any sign of surprise. Looking up from his phone, he made eye contact with her and smiled, "Why, Ms. Moreland. Good to see you again."

I doubt that. "You're kind of far from home aren't you, Mr. Noble?"

"It's not too far, really."

"How's Frank tonight?"

"I think he's getting anxious to get out of that bed. I know I would be."

"I thought you told me you had not talked to Frank Lester since college."

"I hadn't. But then you told me what happened to him." Trace slid his phone into the back pocket of his blue jeans. "I thought the decent thing to do was to come pay my respects."

"I see," she said skeptically.

A look of disappointment crossed his face. "You don't sound like you believe me."

His voice was whiny. She half expected him to pout out his bottom lip.

"If you were in my shoes you might find it a bit suspicious."

"Well maybe," he conceded, "but if you were in my shoes and you found out that an old college teammate was in the hospital, you'd probably go see him even if you hadn't had contact for years."

"I would if it was a teammate I had a positive relationship with. Did you two have a positive relationship?"

"We did."

"That is not what I have been told."

Trace knit his eyebrows as if her statement was a complete surprise. "Who told you different?"

"That's not pertinent."

Trace held up his hands in mock surrender. "Excuse me. I didn't know I was asking a touchy question."

Nattie held her ground.

"Look," he said gently, "I didn't mean anything by that. I know this is serious and I mean no disrespect to you, so I'll tell you the truth. Frank and I were numbers one and two on that pitching staff. We had our angry

169

moments. We're both fierce competitors. I was the ace and he was the youngster who wanted to be the ace. But believe me, I wanted him on that team." He whistled. "We probably would have won Nationals if he had been with us for the spring semester."

"He must have been surprised to see you then."

"I called first, you know, to see if there was anything special he wanted me to bring."

He waited for her to ask.

She waited for him to continue.

"He wanted a cheeseburger and a cold one."

"So you came bearing gifts and he was glad to see you."

"He would have taken a cold one from Bin Laden tonight."

"Are you comparing yourself to Bin Laden, Mr. Noble?"

Trace smiled and leaned uncomfortably close to her. "Are you trying to bust my chops, Ms. Moreland? I gave you my alibi. What more do you want?"

"Do you mean the picture you e-mailed me?"

"Of course. You got it, didn't you?"

"I did. It's a very interesting picture of a grapefruit."

Shuffling his feet like a five-year-old who just got caught, he confessed, "I knew you'd figure that out eventually, but really, you have to believe me, I had that procedure. I just don't have any of the records. I send everything to my insurance company as soon as I get it. I'll have the real records for you in a couple of days. It was a stupid thing to do, I know. I just didn't want you to waste any more time on me while the real bad guy was getting away. I was going to tell you the truth when I got the insurance records."

"I'll look forward to getting those records."

"And you will," he said crossing his heart with his fingertip. "I promise." Cocking his head, he grinned and asked, "So are we friends again?"

What? she thought as she recoiled.

"OK," he said backing up again. "That was too much, wasn't it? I'm sorry. It just bothers me to be on bad terms with anyone."

"We are not on bad terms, Mr. Noble. We are not on any terms at all. I am a private investigator, and I have been hired to do a job. You are a peripheral person in that investigation. I didn't consider you a serious suspect until you sent me that bogus picture of your heart." Holding up her hand, she cut him off from responding and continued, "I seriously doubt that you would be visiting Frank Lester if there was a possibility that he would suspect you, so I guess your story rings true."

His shoulders relaxed, and he opened his mouth to speak, but her finger in his face stopped him.

"But, Mr. Noble, you wasted my time with that picture. And I do not appreciate having my time wasted."

"Feisty," he said in a sing-songy voice.

Really, she thought, you're going to hit on me now? "You know what? I'm tired and visiting hours are over so I'm going to call it a day. If you'll excuse me, I'll be heading home."

"By all means." He bowed.

She walked to the door without looking back and reminded herself that being a jerk did not make him guilty.

By the time she had walked to her car, exited the garage, and descended the hill, the yellow Thunderbird was no longer there.

CHAPTER 35

HENRY CALLS

Crossing Abingdon on Valley Drive allowed her to bypass all of the traffic lights on Main Street. As she was finally cutting over to Main her phone rang. The ring was an excerpt from "Season of the Witch," so she knew who it was.

"Hello, Mother," she said.

"Hi, honey. What are you up to?"

"I'm on the job, Mom. Is there something you wanted?" *Wait for it.*

"I just wanted to touch bases with you. Since we didn't get together yesterday—"

There it is. Guilt dart. Direct hit if I had not seen it coming.

"I'd thought I check on you and see how you are doing."

"I'm doing great, Mom. Where's Lionel tonight?"

"He's at a meeting, but that's not why I'm calling."

"Oh I know that, Mom." *It's just that when he's not there to entertain you, you get bored and think of me.*

"Tell me about the case you're working on."

"I can't do that, Mom, but I can tell you that I'm in my car driving home from Abingdon."

"Abingdon? What took you to Abingdon?"

A text from Henry Quayle beeped in.

"Nothing exciting. I had to check on an alibi at a nursing home and then I stopped by the hospital to get some information about a patient. I keep telling you that real detective work is nothing like the old Sam Spade movies."

"What about the time the big guy attacked you in the bar?"

"That!" she almost shouted. "That was a publicity stunt arranged by your idiot son."

"Well I thought it was exciting."

Nattie involuntarily rolled her eyes. It was not what her mother said; it was how she said it, as if she had been ridiculed for her thought and she was still standing by it albeit as a victim. *Guilt dart. Direct hit. Didn't see it coming.*

"Really, Mom, most of what I do is wait. And when I'm done waiting, I go all over the place to check out details. Excitement is almost never part of the equation."

"I just want to be part of your life, Natalie."

Another direct hit. They're coming too fast. Time to eject. "Listen, Mom. I just got a text from the man I saw at the nursing home, so I need to get it before I get out of Abingdon. I may have to circle back."

"Call me tomorrow?"

"Sure, and we can set up a date for Italian ice," Nattie promised. Sometimes promises like that gave relief from the guilt darts. Promises like that were always followed by resentment because it never felt as if they were made freely.

The text from Henry Quayle read, "Call me NOW!!!!!"

Waiting until she reached the Perkins parking lot at exit seven Nattie returned the call to Henry Quayle.

"Were you just driving on Valley Drive in Abingdon?" Henry spoke hurriedly, as if he were short of breath.

"I was about fifteen minutes ago. Why? Is something wrong?"

"You were being followed."

Nattie immediately looked around to see if anyone had followed her into the parking lot.

"Where are you now?" he asked.

"At Perkins. In the parking lot. No one followed me in here." Getting out of the car, she surveyed her surroundings. "Are you sure?"

"Have you examined the contents of the envelope I gave you?"

"Not yet, why?"

"Do it and call me back."

"Wh—" Nattie realized he had hung up before she could finish her question.

She had thoroughly enjoyed every aspect of owning her iPhone. That is, she enjoyed every aspect until now. What she wanted to do now was slam it down. Hammerin' Hank had frightened her, then hung up.

I'd like to hang him up, she told herself as retrieved her bag from the backseat and headed inside. She asked for a booth next to the window so she could watch the parking lot on the remote chance it was not Henry Quayle's brain injury acting up.

After ordering she settled back and stared at the brown envelope on the table. The coffee urn came quickly. She sweetened her cup, took a long sip, and, when she was convinced her anxiety was under control, opened the envelope. She withdrew a thin stack of pages.

The first picture was a close-up of her parked car. The second picture was of her parked car from a distance. She could tell by the diagonal parking in the middle of the street that it was taken on Broad Street in Kingsport when she had visited Trace Noble.

You followed me to Kingsport, she said to the Henry Quayle she imagined sitting across from her.

The next picture was of traffic along Broad Street. Nattie held the picture up and studied it more closely. She could find nothing alarming or even familiar in the shot. The same was true of the next three pages.

Finally she came to a picture of a car she recognized. The picture was taken such that only the edge of the passenger side showed, but it was clearly a Mango-colored Jeep Wrangler Unlimited. Beau Robinette had a Mango-colored Jeep Wrangler Unlimited. It was an unusual color for an uncommon car, but it didn't have to be Beau's car. It could belong to someone else. Or it could be his, which doesn't mean he was following me.

The next picture was a close-up of the driver in the Jeep. The glare on the windshield and the shadow inside the car made it difficult to know

174

for sure if it was Beau, but the size of the man and his ponytail were certainly Beau-like.

The next picture showed the driver from the side view. There was no mistaking who it was. Beau.

Nattie noticed that her breathing had become shallow and shorter. She did not notice the tightness in her neck and shoulders, nor did she notice that she was biting her lower lip. The mental gymnastics she was putting herself through to explain away what she was looking at all disappeared when she held the next picture up to view. In this picture Beau was sitting in his vehicle taking pictures with a camera and an enormous zoom lens.

The remaining pages went back into the envelope unexamined as she gathered herself together and made for the exit.

"Are you OK?" asked the waitress standing in the aisle holding a plate of pancakes and sausages and looking confused.

"I have to go make a phone call," she said hurriedly.

"Are you coming back for your food?"

"No, but I left a ten-dollar bill on the table. Keep the change."

"Can I box up your food?" yelled the waitress at her as she made to exit.

Pausing at the door, Nattie glanced back and then came over to where the waitress stood. "Thank you," she said, "I haven't eaten anything since this morning." She rolled one of the sausages up in the top pancake. "I'll just take this, thanks."

"That's his," said the waitress in a meek voice.

Nattie looked in the direction the waitress had nodded. A policeman sitting in the first booth waved back at her and smiled.

"Sorry," she mouthed and made for the door.

"What's this about?" she barked at Henry Quayle. Two bites of the pancake wrap was all she could handle with her stomach in knots.

"You looked at the photos?"

"I did. Why did you follow me to Kingsport?"

"I didn't follow you to Kingsport. I was following him."

Standing next to her car, she scanned the parking lot for Mango-colored Jeeps.

"Ms. Moreland, your client is a dangerous man. I can't prove he has hurt anyone else yet; but he's going to blow, and you do not want to be on the receiving end of it when he does."

"Look, Detective, I don't usually get rattled; but this is really freaking me out."

"Are you armed?"

She felt for the gun at the small of her back just to be sure. "I am."

"I'm sure you will be fine." The remark sounded like something he had said a hundred times to a hundred stalking victims. "Just be careful. Double-check your windows and doors to make sure they are locked."

Beans, she said to herself, remembering that Eli's door was still unlockable.

"And avoid going into isolated spots by yourself."

Great. That won't hamper any of my detective work.

"And Ms Moreland—"

"Yes."

"I passed you on Valley Drive tonight."

The knot in her stomach tightened.

"It was Beau. He was pretty far behind you, but it was him following you. The only reason I caught it was that I was driving in the opposite direction."

Nattie stood frozen. She might have had a past experience with as much fear as she now felt, but she could not recall it. She was aware of little else than the beating of her heart.

"What are you going to do?" Henry asked gently.

"I don't know," she admitted. Hearing her confession out loud took her discouragement to a deeper place.

Time for Nattie seemed to move in slow motion. It also felt like she was watching herself act. Sliding in behind the steering wheel, pulling the seatbelt across her chest, watching the buckle latch, and squirming farther into her seat—she performed all these actions with a level of awareness normally foreign to her. Placing both hands on the steering wheel, she leaned forward. *Come on, girl, get a grip*, she told herself.

Splitting her attention equally between the road ahead and the rearview mirror meant maintaining a speed under twenty-five miles an

176

hour, but this did not keep her from drifting into the curb several times. When another driver laid hard and long on his horn, she pulled to the side of the road to coach herself again. *You never saw Beau's Jeep tonight. You are just letting Henry Quayle's attitude toward him get in your head. There's probably an explanation for those pictures and you won't know until you check it out. That's what YOU do. So get your head straight and do your job. You are two miles from home. No one is following you. Just go home, jam a chair under your backdoor, clear the house, and lock it down. Then tomorrow take those photos and shove them in Beau Robinette's face.*

The coaching worked. Putting her gun on the passenger's seat she laughed out loud. "I've got a gun," she yelled as she began driving again.

Her bravado lasted precisely as long as it took her to glance in her rearview mirror again. Driving closely behind her was a Mango-colored Jeep.

The Subaru Forester lurched forward as she pressed the accelerator to the floor and drove past the entrance to her neighborhood. Her failure to shake the Jeep after several sharp turns confirmed that she was being followed. Her instinct was to drive directly to the police station. The Jeep followed her to Martin Luther King Boulevard, but when she turned off on Anderson Street to go to the police station, the Jeep did not follow her. She watched it go by and, seeing it from the side, realized it was not Beau's four-door Jeep, but a two-door model with a University of Tennessee orange paint job, which looked like Mango under the dimly lit street lights outside her neighborhood.

The realization made her laugh again. "You're lucky I didn't shoot you," she chortled in the direction of the orange Jeep. "That paint job would have been my defense." She laughed all the way through her U-turn. It was fun to make fun of UT fans; they all took it so seriously. And right now she desperately needed something funny to throw her excess energy at.

Fifteen uneventful minutes later, Nattie shut and locked her front door. All the cars on the street she recognized and could match with their respective houses. A quick survey of the front room and the dining room while heading straight for the back door off the kitchen triggered no alarms in her. Jamming a chair under the knob secured that entry point, and she turned her attention to the windows. As she checked the window

177

over the sink, which faced out the side of the house, she saw the Mango-colored four-door Jeep. The sight triggered a double-take. She strained across the counter to make sure it was not another UT fan parked around the corner, but there was no mistaking the vehicle this time. Immediately, she placed the gun she had been carrying on the counter next to the sink and took out her phone to call 911.

Before Nattie could turn it on, the phone was knocked from her hand by someone standing directly behind her. The action made her jump but not before she felt something tighten around her neck. The rope was already too tight as she grabbed at it, desperately trying to get a finger between it and her throat. Giving that up, she swung her elbow around, but the person holding the rope was too strong. She thought her head would pop off as she was shoved forward and then quickly jerked backward. The whiplash caused her to feel dizzy. As she fought to regain her equilibrium, she felt the attacker's breath getting closer to her neck. Then he put his tongue on her. She tried to squeeze her head and right shoulder together to force his face away. He just laughed and shook her again.

"Go ahead and fight," he whispered in her ear while he tightened the rope even more. "That makes it more fun."

She clutched at the rope again, but it was still too tight.

A deeper level of panic swept over her as she felt his hand slide around her midsection. When he reached her belt buckle, her instincts took over, causing her to flail ineffectually. Then a moment of clarity helped her remember what she had been taught in self-defense class. Lifting her right leg she stomped down as hard as she could on top of her assailant's foot.

She heard him scream out in pain and listened as it transitioned into anger. With a frenzied growl he lifted her off her heels and slung her backward. Her head bounced off the floor twice; once when she hit and a second time when he landed on her. She could feel her head being jerked back and forth again. She clutched frantically at the cord around her neck again. Then, against her will, she stopped struggling.

178

CHAPTER 36

IN THE HOSPITAL

"No! Absolutely not!" declared Ingrid O'Brien. "Hasn't she already been through enough?"

"Yes, ma'am," answered the Bristol, Tennessee, police officer from the doorway of Nattie's hospital room.

From her bed Nattie could not see who her mother was talking to; but recognizing his voice, she called out, "Officer Early, is that you?"

Ingrid glared at him as he sidestepped her and entered the room. "It is. It's good to see you with your eyes open. How are you feeling?"

"She's had a concussion. How do you think she's doing?" snapped Ingrid.

"Mother, would you go to the cafeteria and get me a decaf coffee?"

Ingrid huffed. "You want me to leave, right?"

"Thank you, Mother."

Ingrid picked up her purse from the chair under the television and walked slowly to the door, head held high, her jaw extended. "I'll be back in fifteen minutes." She said it without looking to see if the audience was attending her exit. It was.

"I'm guessing that means she's wants me gone after fifteen minutes."

"Yes, that's my mom. Subtle, isn't she?"

"I think she's trying to protect you."

"Oh, she is, but she has another agenda too. She doesn't think I'm in the right occupation."

John Early raised his eyebrows. "Well, it's true you come up unconscious a whole lot more than most folks."

"Twice," she said holding up two fingers. "Were you there for both of them?"

"If it's only been twice, then I've been there for all of them."

In a softer tone she said, "Thank you."

He smiled.

"What can you tell me about it?" she asked almost pleading.

"What do you remember?"

"I remember taking my phone out to call 911 and then he grabbed me from behind. We struggled. Hitting the floor is the last thing I remember."

Early took a folder from under his arm and handed it to her, "Can you identify this man?"

Nattie opened the folder. What she saw startled her, immediately reminding her of the stiffness in her neck. She grimaced as she massaged the back of her neck. "Trace Noble. Why?"

"Can you think of a reason he would have attacked you?"

Nattie squinted. "Excuse me? He attacked me? It was him?"

"It was."

"Are you sure?"

"Absolutely. It was Mr. Noble. We found him lying next to you when we arrived. You were both unconscious. His concussion is worse than yours, by the way. I was not the first on the scene; but when we got the 911 call, I realized it was you so I followed."

"I'm confused. Who made the 911 call?"

"That kid."

"What kid?"

"The kid from the other night. The one we brought to your house."

"Eli? He called 911?"

"He did more than that. According to what he told the officer who interviewed him, he heard a noise and got your baseball bat from the closet to check it out. When he walked into the kitchen he found Noble on top of you with a rope around your neck."

180

"He saved me. Eli, the thirteen-year-old kid, saved me."

"Yes, he did. He had a very busy night."

"What does that mean?"

"Do you remember why we picked him up that night I called you?"

"What he told me was that some homeowner over on Pinehurst Street accused him of going through his garbage."

"That's right. And then, earlier the same night as your attack, that same homeowner left his car in his driveway with the window down. And well." John Early looked down, shuffled awkwardly.

"What did he do?" asked Nattie.

"I don't now if he did it or not, but Eli was everyone's first thought. He had an alibi; he was at your house. After his heroism that night, I wasn't going to pursue it."

"What did you think he did?"

"Someone took advantage of that open window and used the front seat of the car as a toilet."

CHAPTER 37

HENRY QUAYLE IN HOSPITAL

Nattie's neck was still sore, especially if she moved too far or too quickly, but by the second day of her hospital stay her headache was pretty well gone. Ingrid had come early and dropped off a large coffee along with a copy of the *Bristol Herald Courier* opened to the story of her attack. Ingrid tapped the paper with her finger and said, "Is this the kind of life you want to live? What if you had children in your house when that cretin showed up?"

"I don't have children, Mother."

Ingrid threw up her arms in despair. "And you won't, either, if this is how you run your life."

Nattie watched as her mother opened a compact and checked her lipstick. In the not-too-distant past, the scene would have brought a wave of feelings ranging from disappointment to disgust, but not this time. Maybe it was Nattie's change in attitude toward women like Randi, buxom women whom she had previously referred to as sluts, teases, or hoes. Nattie had come to realize that she and others like her virtually abandoned women like Randi, leaving them isolated and friendless in a world where attracting men was simple—they were merely making their way with the resources available to them. "I don't need a man to take care of me," Randi had said. "I just know my way around them."

Ingrid O'Brien was not the same kind of voluptuous woman that Randi was; but she was attractive, and she did know her way around men. To Nattie's nearly constant embarrassment, Ingrid behaved as if she needed a man to take care of her. It was not that she did need a man to take care of her. It was that she had been treated like a princess for much of her life and that she had come to accept such treatment as the natural order of life. With that conditioning, how could anyone blame her for wanting that for her daughter?

Nattie sighed. She tired of blaming her mother for that anymore.

"Mother," Nattie said softly. She patted the edge of her bed. "Come sit here a minute."

Ingrid looked surprised, but did as she was told. Once seated, she held Nattie's hand in her lap.

"Thanks, Mom," Nattie said. That's got to be the pain medication, she told herself as she teared up.

"Oh honey, you don't have to thank me." Ingrid wiped Nattie's cheek with the back of her hand. "I'm your mother."

"I don't think I told you how much I appreciated you."

Ingrid cocked her head to the side.

"No, Mom, I mean it. You were young and beautiful—"

"Oh stop," Ingrid interrupted.

"It could not have been easy to start life over with two kids to take care of. And you did it."

"I didn't think you approved of my marriage to Lionel."

"You made sure Kevin and I were taken care of, and I appreciate it. I'm sorry if I made it hard for you and Lionel. I just thought you changed too much for him."

"Changed? What are you talking about, honey?"

"Well," Nattie held her Franciscan cross away from her neck. "Your interest in Saint Francis, for one thing."

Ingrid eyed the necklace. "Is that mine?"

"It's mine, mom; but if you want it, you can have it. I'll get another."

"Was that with the other things I left out for you?"

Nattie was not sure she heard correctly. "What do you mean? Are you talking about all the Saint Francis stuff you threw away when Lionel asked you to marry him?"

"I never threw any of that away. I left it in a box for you on the kitchen table."

"That box was on top of the garbage." Nattie then began to piece together the memories of that day. "Kevin was putting a large Lego race car together and had it spread all over the kitchen table—. Oh my gosh, Mom, I feel horrible. I've always blamed you for abandoning that stuff. I'll bet he put your box on top of the garbage can."

Ingrid just smiled.

"I'm sorry, Mom."

Hopping down from the bed, Ingrid brushed the wrinkles from her slacks. Then she leaned over on her tiptoes and kissed Nattie on the forehead. "Thank you. You don't owe me an apology, but I appreciate it that you think you do." She stepped back. "I know you wish I was more independent like you. But I'm not."

Nattie opened her mouth to object but Ingrid placed her finger on Nattie's lips and continued, "I don't want you to be like me; I just want you to be happy."

Who are you, wondered Nattie, *and what have you done with my mother?* Aloud she said, "I'm glad to hear you say that, Mom, because I'm a detective; and this case notwithstanding, I'm good at it."

"Of course you're good at it." The conviction in Ingrid's voice, though unexpected, was real enough. "You would be good at whatever you did."

"Detective work is what I do. It makes me happy, Mom."

Ingrid looked at her watch. "Look at that. I've got to go. I have an appointment for a massage."

"Thank you," Nattie called after the departing figure.

Without looking back, Ingrid waved over her shoulder. "I'll be back this afternoon."

The story in the paper consisted of three paragraphs on page five. She was referred to as "Local detective Natasha McMorales." "Oh that's great," she said out loud as she read her name. The paper's account of the incident reported that Trace Noble of Kingsport had attacked her in her home and that a "Good Samaritan" had intervened on her behalf.

The reference to Eli, a thirteen-year-old, as the "Good Samaritan" made her chuckle. Of course, she realized. The police could not give the name of a minor to the newspaper. She lifted her coffee cup in a toast to the Good Samaritan. "Thanks, Eli; you really saved me."

After taking a drink from her cup she chuckled. "I guess there's no getting rid of you now."

"No getting rid of who?" asked Henry Quayle from the doorway.

The question startled her, which reminded her once again that her neck was not fully recovered. "Come in, Detective," she said as she rubbed her neck.

"I half expected to find you in a neck brace," he said as he took a position at the foot of the bed. "They have to be extra careful with neck injuries."

"I've had every kind of X-ray you could imagine. We're pretty sure my injuries are muscular."

"You see," he continued, "It's really the spinal cord."

"What brings you by, Detective?" she asked before he could begin his lesson on the spinal cord.

"I wanted to check on you and to thank you in person."

"Thank me for what?" she asked.

"For solving the Frank Lester case, naturally. You were right; I was wrong. It wasn't Beau Robinette after all."

"This may sound like a strange question, but who was it?"

Henry's laughter sounded more like a snort. "You solved it, but I guess no one has told you that yet. I suppose you were just defending yourself, but the gold chain you yanked off Mr. Noble turned out to be the key piece of evidence."

"I yanked a chain off of his neck?" Nattie asked slowly.

"You don't remember that, do you?"

"I don't remember much about what happened."

"I'm not surprised. In extreme circumstances like that, instincts take over. You probably grabbed at anything and everything you could while you were struggling. When the police found you, there was a broken gold chain with an Ace of Diamonds pendant on it. It matches Frank Lester's tattoo, and it has his name engraved on the back. His wife verified that it

185

is Frank's necklace, and Frank himself confirmed that it had been taken from him the night he was attacked."

"And Trace Noble had it?"

"Yes. Frankie boy couldn't contain himself when he found out who it was. He said he was going to kill Trace with an ice pick as soon as he could walk. Can you imagine saying that to a couple of cops?"

"What did you do?"

"Of course we were obligated to inform Mr. Noble that he had been threatened. And then the floodgates opened up. Noble implicated Lester in several assaults; Lester implicated Noble in extortion. I'll tell you, it was really something. It will take us weeks, maybe months, to verify everything these two idiots said about each other. When this is all done, neither of them is going to be a free man for a long, long time. And it all started with that necklace you took from Trace Noble."

"Wow!" Nattie exclaimed, not knowing what else to say.

"It's a far cry better than 'wow!' Ms. McMorales. There are going to be some rewards coming your way when the dust settles from all of this."

"Wow!" she said again.

CHAPTER 38

NATTIE CONFRONTS BOO

"Why me?" asked Boo.

It had been three days since the attack in her kitchen, two of which were spent in the hospital, so Nattie was taking things slowly. She was barely conscious when the paramedics got her to the hospital, and the doctors had been concerned about brain damage. Still, she was determined to tend to the unfinished business of the Frank Lester case. She had been released on the condition that she spend the next week at her mother's house, a condition that delighted Ingrid and required Kevin act as her chauffeur.

Kevin had made sure that her schedule was clear. But for Nattie there was one piece of business that would not wait. The story the police gave her when they came to her hospital room did not satisfy her. She wanted the truth and she wanted it now. Beau agreed to meet her at her office.

"I'm asking you for several reasons, Boo. It never made sense to me why you hired me in the first place."

"I told you. I had extra money from the sale of the Never Tell and I wanted to do something good with it."

"When I first talked to Nathan at Our House you referred to Frank Lester as the guy who got his leg broken with a baseball bat."

Boo shrugged.

"That information hadn't been released to the public yet." She watched his big grin morph into seriousness. "You couldn't have known it was a baseball bat unless you were there."

His eyes lit up and his grin returned. "The cop who came to question Nathan mentioned the bat." He slapped his knee and laughed out loud. "You were bluffing." Another slap of the knee. "I knew you were good, Natasha."

You're good, too, my friend, she thought as she waited for him to finish enjoying his relief.

"And then there's Eli Anderson."

"Eli Anderson?"

"He's the 'Good Samaritan' the newspaper referred to when they printed the story. He's only thirteen, so the police could not release his name to the press."

Boo scrunched his face. "OK?" he said in a drawn-out way, as if to indicate "So what?"

"Here's the story: Eli was there and saw the whole thing, Trace Noble throwing me around like a rag doll. That's how he described it. And then he rushed out from his hiding place with a baseball bat and knocked Noble unconscious just before he could kill me."

"The kid is a hero. He's got to like that. It'll give him a great reputation."

"He can't tell anyone about that," she said with a sneer. "What do you think would happen to him if Trace Noble discovered it was him?"

"You're right," agreed Boo.

"And there's also the fact that he didn't do it."

"Did he tell you that?"

"No. He lied, though. But the fact is, he isn't strong enough to cause that kind of damage. Besides, the story is that he was hiding in a closet, and that's where he got the baseball bat."

"OK."

"I don't keep a baseball bat in my closet. No, I think he walked in after you were finished and before you left. I think your plan was just to leave. You expected the Good Samaritan story to be the official position, but Eli's getting there messed you up." Nattie leaned forward. "I'm not going to bother asking what you said to him to get him to back up your story."

Boo sat back in his chair and folded his hands in his lap. His voice was somber. "Why are you telling me all this?"

"That's a good question, Boo. I should be telling all of this to Henry Quayle."

"You should," he agreed, "but you aren't. Why?"

"Well, you saved my life. I figure I owe you something for that."

Boo nodded his head slightly.

"I am curious, though. I think Henry Quayle may have been right about you."

"Oh, he's a fool."

"Maybe so," she conceded, "but he's right about you being a vigilante, isn't he, Boo?"

Boo remained stoically silent.

"You were never prosecuted for that assault in Washington County, but you did it, didn't you? That story you told about the other man stabbing you."

"That's no story; he did stab me."

"But you baited him, didn't you?"

"Look. Natasha, I like you. I like you a lot. But you cannot seriously expect me to continue this conversation."

"I can and do expect that. What are your choices, Boo? I have information and I am asking you to help me decide what to do with it. Do you want to explain or not?"

"If I was the monster you think I am, then I could protect myself by squashing you like a bug."

Nattie smiled. "But you aren't a monster, and I have never believed that for a moment. No, what I think is that you are a monster basher. The monsters you have gone after have all been men who abuse women."

"What do you want?"

"Specifically, I want to know why you went after Frank Lester, and then I want to know why you hired me to find out who did it."

Boo leaned forward and placed his elbows on his knees. "Let's just say, hypothetically, that I had answers for all those questions. What then?"

Nattie shook her head. "There are no guarantees here, Boo. You can either trust me with the answers, or you do not trust me."

Boo sighed and sat back again. "Am I being recorded?"

"Nope."

"OK, then. A while ago a woman came into the Never Tell and said she wanted to buy it. I told her thanks, but no thanks. I still had work to finish on it before I moved on. She said fine and left. A couple of days later she came back and offered me more money. She said she was representing an investment firm out of Memphis and they were in a hurry." He flipped his right hand over. "I turned her down again. That's when it got ugly. It was a Thursday afternoon, a little bit before four o'clock, and I get this phone call. It was a man's voice. I didn't recognize it. Anyway, he said, 'Someone here wants to talk to you.' The next voice I heard was my niece's." Boo's big hand tightened into a fist. "Emma is fifteen. Two men grabbed her in the parking lot of her school; they put a black bag over her head and abducted her. 'Uncle Beau,' she said. She calls me Beau instead of Boo. 'They say they will leave me alone if you sell your place to that lady.'"

"She must have been terrified."

"Not Emma. The next thing she said was, 'but I don't want you to sell anything to these creee—' I think she was going to say creeps but they took the phone away from her and one of them told me to 'be smart and do what I was told without involving the police.'"

"What did you do?"

Boo shrugged his shoulders. "What could I do? They had my niece. They had the upper hand and I wasn't going to do anything that would put Emma in danger." He paused before continuing, "They dropped her off behind the dairy and were long gone by the time she got the bag off her head. But I couldn't ignore the threat that they could get to her any time they wanted."

"Was she OK?"

"That's a tricky question to answer. She's a tough kid, but that had to be scary. So when she acted like it was nothing, I wondered if she was telling us everything."

"She was protecting you?" Nattie wondered out loud.

"No, Well, maybe she was doing that too. But mostly I think she was going through the stages of rape trauma."

The image of Trace Noble's hand on her belt buckle intruded into Nattie's thoughts. "Oh my goodness. Was she raped?"

190

"She was abducted, threatened, and groped." Boo swallowed hard. "They were just thugs strong-arming a business deal until they did that."

Nattie was silent while Boo looked down and struggled to breathe. "It was a chicken-shit thing to do."

"It was a chicken-shit thing to do," she agreed.

"And the penalty for chicken-shit has to be stiffer than the penalty for mere crime. You understand that, don't you?"

"Of course I understand. And I agree a hundred percent."

"But—"

"But I don't think it would work well if we let every angry uncle stiffen the penalty."

"And we don't let every angry uncle stiffen the penalty," he observed. Then grinning, he added, "Maybe we should let someone else's uncle stiffen the penalty."

"I don't want to debate that with you now, Boo. I just want to know how you got from that phone call to my kitchen."

He nodded. "Well I sold the Never Tell the next day and agreed to stay on as the manager on a week-to-week basis."

"In an attempt to find out who was behind all of this, I assume."

He nodded. "That turned out to be a dead end, though. The woman was just a realtor; she didn't know who she was working for. It was all handled out of Memphis, but when I tracked the company down, it was a dummy front."

"But if money passed hands, there would be a paper trail somewhere. We could have traced down the buyer."

"I know; but it wasn't the buyer I cared about."

"It was the creeps who took your niece."

"Exactly, and as luck would have it a better trail to them walked right into my tavern." Boo emphasized this point as if he was the author of the story and was proud of how cleverly he had just twisted the plot.

Nattie played the appreciative audience by asking, "What happened?"

"Well, Emma couldn't see very much because of the black bag over her head. She did, however, see the hands of the two men. It was not the man who groped her but he was there and he held her while it happened." Boo rubbed his fingertip across the knuckles on his left hand. "The guy who held her had four aces tattooed on his fingers."

"Frank Lester," contributed Nattie.

"Yes, and there he was sitting at my bar, making jokes and having a good time. Then he got a phone call that got him all excited. He asked me for a pad of paper and he wrote down an address while he said, 'and you're sure this is her lover,' and then, 'I'm busy tonight, but you can bet your ass he'll be seeing me tomorrow evening.' Well, when he took the top sheet from that pad it was easy to shade the next page with a pencil and discover exactly where he was going to be the next night."

"Our House."

"I didn't recognize the name enough to remember that Nathan and you had come out to Barley Corners to talk to me about that murder in my parking lot. I just knew that Bozo was going to be there. And since he was after someone, I figured he would probably bring his partner with him."

"But he didn't."

"No, he didn't. He came by himself. But he was coming back; I was sure of that."

"So you asked Nathan for a job as a bartender so you could be there if Frank and his partner showed back up?"

"He remembered my red beans and rice and insisted that I do a little cooking too. I was only interested in a bartending job."

"So you would be out front if they showed up."

"That's right."

"But you didn't wait for them. You went after Frank before his buddy showed up," observed Nattie. "But why?"

"I was talking with Randi, Frank Lester's wife."

"I remember who she is," said Nattie unsympathetically.

"Well, I got to thinking that it was strange that Lester just threatened Nathan. It dawned on me that he must have a plan to draw Nathan out."

"You thought he was going to turn on Randi," guessed Nattie.

"Well, he was abusing her and it was getting worse. She had decided she was going to leave him. I knew if she was ever at risk for being killed, it would be when she was leaving him."

And that was all you needed to hear to turn loose the dogs of war, thought Nattie.

"So I did what needed doing. That meant I had to find the other one, though, the one I was really after, some other way."

"So you hired me to flush him out," accused Nattie.

192

"No."

"Yes you did. You used me like a bird dog."

As Boo shook his head, a slight smile formed. "Well, I suppose I did. I meant no disrespect; but you have to admit, it worked."

"Yeah, it worked." And it nearly got me killed. "We flushed out a creep, but how do you know he is the same creep who groped your niece?"

"She saw his hand, too."

"The FIRE tattoo."

Boo looked sheepish. "When you went to interview Noble, I followed you and put a bug in his car. I've been listening to him for the past few days."

"And?"

"And he called Frank right after you left. He was upset that Frank's grandstanding for a woman—only he was more crude than that—put their 'other business' at risk. He said Frank should get better soon because he was the only one he could count on for more 'delicate' situations."

"That evidence is what my lawyer stepfather would call circumstantial."

"And that's why it is sometimes better to get things done before the lawyers get involved. Besides, I have one more piece of circumstantial evidence. Trace also told Frank that they needed to start working again since the Barley Corners deal had gone bad."

"I thought you did what they wanted. You sold your place, right?"

"That part went the way they wanted. My best guess is that they bought my place because it was on the river. The county commission had considered sanctioning riverboat gambling and Trace and Frank wanted to be the first to cash in. But the county commission crossed them up."

"Was the tattoo enough to convince you that you got the right guy?"

Boo just looked at her. The answer was obvious.

"OK, tell me this. Why were you following me tonight?"

"I wasn't following you. I was following Trace."

Nattie shuddered. "You followed him here."

"I did."

"You saved my life."

"I did," he repeated.

She began gently, "I suppose I should thank you." Then, at the thought of what she had just been through, she clinched her teeth. "But you put me in the line of fire."

He smiled sheepishly as she punched him in the right shoulder.

"Tell me about that night, Boo."

"The night Frank Lester was attacked?"

The night you attacked him. "Yes, that night."

"There's nothing to tell other than what you already know. I waited for him in his carport. According to Randi, he keeps his beer out there, so I knew if I waited long enough he'd come out for a beer. Since his car was gone when I got there, I just waited until he came home."

"Go on."

"He walked right by me and never saw me. So I just grabbed him from behind and cut his air off until he went limp. Then I worked him over with a baseball bat."

"What about the pendant?"

"I knew from Randi that it was important to him. He liked to rub it when he got rough. Randi said it gave her the chills because it seemed so erotic."

"Sick," said Nattie with a scowl on her face. "And you took the necklace from him when you, I mean, when he was knocked unconscious."

Boo nodded.

"And that's the broken chain that was in my hand when the police found me."

Boo nodded again.

"Clever."

Through a half smile, he agreed. "I thought so."

"The police never mentioned anything about that chain to me."

"They didn't know," explained Boo. "Frank didn't report that."

"Why not?" Nattie asked before answering it herself. "Because he was planning on executing justice himself."

"That was my thought," confessed Boo.

"Very clever, Boo."

"So, Natasha, now that you have heard my story, what happens next?"

"I'm not sure yet." She squinted at him. "Tell me, Boo, did you know eventually he would be coming after me?"

194

"Not until that night."

"You played that pretty close." Nattie rubbed her hands across her neck where she had been choked.

"I was in there no more than thirty seconds after he came in."

She scowled, "And if you had come ten seconds later we wouldn't be having this conversation right now."

Gritting his teeth, Boo pleaded, "I am real sorry about that. You have to know I never wanted you to get hurt."

"But using me as bait was OK?"

"I know. That was bad. But after I heard all those stories about how you broke the nose of a real big guy at Nathan's bar, I thought you could take pretty good care of yourself."

"Are you serious? That's why you hired me? Because you heard that story from my brother? That's why me?"

CHAPTER 39

DINNER WITH NATHAN

"Do you think you are fully recovered now?" asked Nathan.

The attack in Nattie's kitchen was three weeks earlier. The only lasting injuries to her were strained muscles in her neck that just needed time to heal. Still, she had been shaken, literally and emotionally, and had agreed to stay with her mother for the first ten days after being released from the hospital. Nathan had asked to take her out immediately, but she had put him off a week. Now the week had passed and she could put him off no longer. He chose House on Main in Abingdon for their lunch date.

She rubbed the back of her neck. "Pretty much. It doesn't bother me in bed anymore, so I'm sleeping more normally. The only time it bothers me now is when I have to look back over my right shoulder."

"That makes driving tough."

"It does, but Kevin is still chauffeuring me around."

Nathan sighed. "It's nice to have people around when you need them."

It would have been nice to have had you around when I needed you, Nathan. Although tempted to speak her thoughts out loud, Nattie refrained. Nathan looked too vulnerable. It was not in her to take the open shot at him, even if he deserved it. "It is," she said.

"I'm going to be one of those people you can count on when you need to."

Hearing his pledge felt like a weight pressing on her chest. It made inhaling difficult. A response was necessary, but what to say escaped her. She just wanted to flee. "Nathan, you don't have to—" Luckily, she did not have to finish. The server brought the gazpacho Nathan had ordered when they arrived.

"Beau brought me up here for lunch before he left. To try this and the Hell or High Watermelon beer. I didn't have the beer," Nathan added quickly. "But when I had this soup, I knew I had to bring you here. What do you think?"

Nattie ran her spoon through the liquid. "I've never seen it so creamy. What's this white stuff?"

"Buttermilk sorbet."

"Mmmm," she moaned as she took her first taste. "It's delicious."

"So, tell me. What's new with the case?"

His question had the effect of moving their conversation to a different place. It was a tactic they were both aware of and both preferred.

"Trace Noble is still incarcerated awaiting trial for attacking me. He's also been charged with attacking Frank Lester. The more they dig into his business dealings, the more they are finding to charge him with. It's going to be a long time before he walks among us again."

"That gets me off the hook with Frank Lester, doesn't it?"

"Oh yeah. When the police told him they had recovered his necklace from Trace Noble, Frank threatened to kill him."

"He threatened to kill that Noble fellow right in front of the police?"

Nattie snickered. "He did. And when they told Noble Frank had threatened him, he began to tell them things about Frank that will mean he's going to go away for a long time, too. Apparently, they had been partners in crime for a good while; and when they began telling on each other, it all unraveled. The police are still gathering evidence."

Nathan lifted his spoon to make a toast. "To a better world where the guilty get caught and the innocent go free."

Do you consider Boo innocent? Nattie wondered as she lifted her spoon toward his. *For that matter are you innocent? Am I?* Choosing not to speak at all, she tapped his spoon with her own.

"Did you say 'before Beau left'?" she asked.

"I did. He packed up that pumpkin Jeep of his and moved to Chattanooga a couple of weeks ago."

"Really?"

"Yep. He said I should tell you that if you need him, he's got your back."

Nattie looked away and smiled. Thanks Boo.

"Does that have a special meaning to you?" Nathan must have noticed her shifting in her seat.

"Nope," she lied. "It's just a generic expression."

"Randi's gone too."

"Oh?"

"She called a guy she knew from college and asked for a job. She's in Paris now working as a gofer for a photographer."

"Good for her," Nattie said and she meant it. "Will you miss her?"

Nathan was tentative in his answer. "Would it bother you if I said I will?"

"You know, it would have before. But no, not now."

"I just want you to know, Nattie. There was never anything between Randi and me other than two lonely people spending time together."

"I think your relationship was more than that, Nathan."

"But it wasn't, Nat—"

She cut him off before he could finish. "You don't have to explain. I have no claim on you."

"But I want you to have a claim on me."

She hesitated and then she watched him deflate. It was as if he knew he had said too much.

"Look, Nathan, I'm not sure what kind of future we have. We have a lot of past in the way."

"It wasn't all bad, was it?" he asked with wide puppy eyes.

"It wasn't all bad." She found herself agreeing with him against her will and then amended her answer. "But I am not willing to go back to what was bad."

"Nat, I've been sober for nearly a year. What more can I do?"

Nathan looked desperate to understand what went wrong, to know what to fix. It was the drinking that they had fought about. And it was his irresponsibility, which was also connected to his drinking, that had been

198

the final straw. But his drinking was not the real issue. He was asking for the real issue, and he deserved to know. She wanted to tell him the truth, but it just was not clear enough to her for her to explain it to him.

"I think I need counseling," she blurted out finally.

Nathan pounced on what he thought she said. "I'll go to counseling."

"That's fine, Nathan. But what I said is that I need counseling."

He heard her correctly this time. But what he heard made him sit back and stare at her in confusion.

"I'm glad for you that you are sober now, but I don't want it to be about me."

"But it is about you. I had a problem, and it took losing you to force me to admit it."

"But you have to fix it for you. What will happen if you fix it for me and something goes wrong between us?"

"There hasn't been an 'us' for a long time, and I stayed sober."

"I know. But I'm afraid if we got back together, it would be different."

"How?"

Because right now the threat of losing me is part of your sobriety, but who knows what will happen if the threat is gone. The thought was too private and placed too much importance on her for her to say it out loud. "I don't know, Nathan; it would just be different."

"You've made that clear."

The remark stung, and Nattie shifted uncomfortably. Is sarcasm the way you want to go now?

"I'm sorry," he said after watching her react. "You don't deserve my frustration."

"Thank you." Wow, Nathan, you made that about me not you. Maybe we could have a future.

"I just want things to be different."

Nattie exhaled slowly. "Here's what it comes down to, Nathan. When you were in my life, my life was about making your life work."

"I never asked you to put your life on hold for me."

"You never asked, but you made it necessary."

Pressing his lips together, he swallowed hard.

She knew she had hurt him more than she intended. "It's not just you. I'm the one making those choices. And that's why I'm going to go to counseling just for me."

Nathan nodded, thankful that he was not being blamed, but confused about what he could do. "Where does that leave us, then?"

"For now there is no 'us.' There can't be an 'us' until there's a 'me.'"

"That's a crock."

The suddenness of his anger startled her.

"I mean it, Nattie. 'There is no "us" until there is a "me."' Where did you get that?"

"You wanted an explanation. That's the best I've got."

"Well, it sounds like a brush-off to me. If you don't have any feelings for me, I'd prefer you say so to that kind of psycho-mumbo-jumbo."

"Maybe there is no future for us," she said defiantly.

"Maybe there isn't," he agreed.

The ride home was in silence.

"Good night," she said as she got out of his truck. He did not speak, but he waited until she was inside before driving away.

Her front room seemed dark and heavy as she stood by her front window and watched his taillights disappear around the corner.

Without turning on a light she plopped down in her cushy chair. Holding her bag on her lap, she reached in for her phone and felt a package. There was enough light from the streetlamp outside for her to tell that it was wrapped in the colored cartoon section from a Sunday paper. Nathan did not believe in gift wrap. He preferred using funny papers. He must have placed the package in her bag when she was in the ladies' room.

She took the package to the kitchen where she turned on a light and tore open the wrap. Inside was a cookbook. She noted the author, Delia Davenport, before putting the book down on the countertop.

"What are you doing, Nathan?" she said out loud even though she was alone. The choice of Delia Davenport was touching, but she was in no mood to be "touched." "Do you think a sentimental gesture is all it takes to win me over?" she growled. With a trace of anger she picked up the book and glanced around the kitchen for a place to throw it. Finding none, she decided just to stick it on the shelf with the other cookbooks.

Attempting to place the new cookbook on the shelf above her sink she discovered that lifting her arm above her head was another painful reminder of her neck injury. The pain made the decision for her; she would leave it on the counter for now. Looking closer she saw the full title for the first time: Delia Davenport's Do's & Don'ts of Dessert.

The title was intriguing to her. Not bad, Nathan, she admitted. Her anger quickly returned as she remembered that she did not want to be tempted by him. But anger was not an emotion she could hold for long. Picking up the book again, she ran her fingers across the cover. As if in a trance she opened the book. Taped to the inside of the cover was a slug; and underneath it Nathan had written, "Hoping for magic to happen again."

THE END, NOT

CHECK OUT OTHER TITLES AT

csthompsonbooks.com

*AUTHOR'S BLOG

*PHOTOS

*AUTHOR'S BIO

*EXCERPTS OF FUTURE BOOKS

*SHORT VIDEOS OF AUTHOR READING

*MUSIC OF THE MONTH

Made in the USA
Charleston, SC
27 April 2015